Time Trap

Time Trap

FaSt FoRWaRD

DIRECTED BY IAN BONE
CINEMATOGRAPHY BY JOBI MURPHY

delacorte press

Published by
Delacorte Press
an imprint of
Random House Children's Books
a division of Random House, Inc.
New York

Visit us on the Web! www.randomhouse.com/teens
Educators and librarians, for a variety of teaching tools,
visit us at www.randomhouse.com/teachers

Library of Congress Cataloging-in-Publication Data
Bone, Ian.
Time trap / Ian Bone ; with storyboards by Jobi Murphy.
p.   cm. — (Fast forward ; #2)
Summary: Kaz is the star of the latest Vidz movie, which transports her to a world much
like her own in which she has helped invent a time machine, but she interferes with the
time line while trying to identify and stop the villain.
ISBN 0-385-73211-2 (trade) — ISBN 0-385-90241-7 (glb)
[1. Video recordings—Fiction. 2. Space and time—Fiction. 3. High schools—Fiction.
4. Schools—Fiction. 5. Adventure and adventurers—Fiction.] I. Murphy, Jobi, ill. II.
Title.

PZ7.B63697Ti 2005
[Fic]—dc22
2004043913

The text of this book is set in 11-point ITC Officina Serif.

Book design by Kenny Holcomb

Printed in the United States of America

February 2005

10   9   8   7   6   5   4   3   2   1

BVG

1

Scene one

Fade in . . .

Kaz Murneau looked at the black emptiness of her wallet and sighed. There wasn't a single cent to be found in it. Not even the faint odor of money. She watched as her friends, Hamish and Bo, reached for ice-cold cans of soft drink from the refrigerator at the canteen. It had been a long day at Capra Video High School. First the air-conditioning had broken down in their classroom. Then they'd had to stand in the hot shade for hours as their camera teacher, Mr. Bolex, showed them how to frame up camera shots for different dramatic effects. How could she concentrate on low-angle shots, close-ups, and wide shots when her skin was melting?

And now she couldn't even afford a cold drink. It wasn't fair! She'd been frying all day. Kaz glared at her friends. She'd do anything to get a drink . . . *anything*!

She'd fight a hundred ninjas guarding a drinks truck.

She'd storm a cola factory.

She'd rob a bank!

 Kaz snapped back to reality and smiled grimly. Some of Bolex's droning must have actually sifted through to her brain. He'd probably even be proud of her if he could have seen all the camera shots she'd imagined.

Bo and Hamish were lining up to pay for their drinks. It was okay for them, they had pocket money. Ever since her dad's business went broke, Kaz's ready supply of money had dried to a trickle. She closed her useless wallet and threw it into her bag. No way would she borrow any more money. She already owed her friends big-time. Besides, she still had *some* pride left.

Bo walked past with his drink, pausing in front of her to slam it down.

"Not thirsty?" he said, letting out a long belch.

Kaz shook her head, watching her friend crush the empty can and toss it into the bin. She suddenly felt hotter, and wondered if Bolex had given them heatstroke, making them stand outside like that. Not that he'd ever notice—he was too in love with the sound of his own voice.

"This is a camera setup I used in the Powers, class. . . ."

"The Powers" were the famous Austin Powers movies, and for a while Kaz and her classmates had believed that Bolex had actually been the cameraman on those movies. Then Hamish went and checked all the credits and found out that Bolex had only been something like seventh assistant to the assistant, which basically meant he'd made the tea! And now he made poor junior students bake outside while he dribbled on, wearing his corny leather gadget belt that held nothing more than a pocketknife. Not to mention his silver jewelry that poked out from his hairy chest . . .

Yuck! thought Kaz.

"Want some of my drink?" said Hamish. He was standing in front of her, holding out his can. "I haven't had much, so there's not too many boy germs. . . ."

Kaz's hand twitched. All she had to do was reach out and take it. She could even see herself drinking: a close-up of the can going to her lips. The sound effect of herself gulping greedily. Another close-up of her throat as the cool liquid goes down . . .

"No thanks," she said, sitting at one of the canteen tables.

Her mouth felt dead dry, but she wasn't going to let them know. After all, she was popular Kaz, not some pathetic whinger. Hadn't she always been the one with the money before her dad's troubles? She bought drinks for her friends, not the other way around. The fact that she had no money was just a minor glitch. Her dad would get his business going again. One day . . .

Kaz sighed.

Hamish pulled a newspaper from his bag and held it up. "Check this out."

"It's a newspaper," said Kaz.

Hamish managed a half smile. "Thanks for that brilliant observation," he said. "I meant, check out the article at the bottom of page one. I think there might be a connection between that story and us. You know, the evil and the Vidz thing . . ."

Bo was nodding, but all Kaz could manage was a sleepy expression. Hamish sighed and spelt it out. "This could be what we'll have to fight in the next Vidz movie," he said.

Kaz held up her hand. "I get it, I get it," she snapped. Her head was too hot to think about evildoings in their city. But she was a Vidz director. And that was the job of Vidz directors, to fight the bad guys. She looked at the newspaper article. The headline read:

FOURTH TEENAGER STEALS EVERYTHING PARENTS OWN!

"Something very weird is going on here," muttered Hamish.

Bo read the headline, then shrugged. "What's so weird about that?" he said. "Teenagers have been taking from their parents for years. . . ."

"Ha ha," said Hamish. "This is different. They actually *rob* them. Something strange happens to these kids. No one can explain it. One day they're your usual teenagers—misunderstood and unloved—the next, they've taken everything from their home."

"Maybe they need the money," said Kaz gloomily.

"No, that's the spookiest thing about it," said Hamish, sitting forward eagerly. "When the cops catch them, the kids don't have any of the money or the stuff they stole. Nothing. And even spookier, they can't remember what they did with it."

"I can't remember what I did with last week's pocket money," said Bo.

"This is more than pocket money," said Hamish. "And it gets worse. It's like their minds have been wiped clean."

"Oh," said Bo. "That does sound kinda evil."

Kaz stretched, taking the newspaper from Hamish and scanning the article. None of the names of the teenagers was familiar to her. They all attended other high schools. "Okay," she said. "This looks pretty horrible to me, too. But what are we gonna do about it"?

"Well . . . that's the thing, isn't it," said Hamish. "We have to wait for the next Vidz."

Kaz rolled her eyes. That was the special feature of being on the Vidz crew. They didn't go out and fight evil, they fought it within a Vidz movie. Hamish had been the first to discover it. He'd been thrown into a movie where *he* was the main character, a hero with a mighty sword who had to fight to save his king.

"This is frustrating," said Kaz. "When will the next Vidz movie happen? And what sort of movie is it? By the look of that newspaper article it will be some kind of horror movie, with a brainsucking monster and zombies walking around."

Bo laughed at Kaz's description, but Hamish had a serious look on his face.

"I don't think we can ever guess what sort of movie a Vidz will be," he said. "All we can do is try to work out how it's connected to us and our real world. . . ."

Kaz's smile slowly melted away. Hamish was always so serious, but he was also right. That was exactly how the Vidz worked. Like a mirror. Beat the bad guy in the Vidz and you exposed evil in the real world.

Then we bring the creeps down, thought Kaz. It had been easy in the first Vidz movie because the mirror was so obvious. The evil Lord Dudley had a magical hold over the king. Hamish defeated Dudley, and before they knew it the credits were rolling, the music was swelling, and they had a happy ending on their hands. Then, back at Capra, they exposed the creepy bursar, Cushing, who was blackmailing the principal of Capra High, Mr. Arbuckle.

It was an especially sweet bust for Kaz, because Cushing had been giving her a hard time, trying to frame her for some robberies. He was once Kaz's dad's business partner, and he hated anyone from the Murneau family, which was outrageous because it was Cushing who had swindled Kaz's dad and made his business go broke in the first place. Cushing had been a real toad. He practically wore a sign saying "I am the bad guy."

"Great," said Kaz. "Not only do we not know what sort of movie the next Vidz will be, but we don't even have any idea which one of us will be the star in it."

"I hope it's not me," said Bo. "I've got too much homework to finish. . . ."

Kaz wanted to smile again, but her lips felt like they'd crack. She wished she'd taken some of Hamish's drink. "That's the part I find hard to get a grip on," she said. "Not knowing who it's going to be. I'd like to prepare myself and stuff. . . . I mean, I've played my Vidz DVD over a million times already, just in case. . . ."

"And?" asked Bo.

"Nothing. The screen is always black. So I guess it's not me who's fighting this evil. . . ."

"And I've played mine, too," said Bo. "Nothing. Nix. Zero."

"Maybe you just have to be patient," said Hamish. "I mean, my money's on you, Kaz. After all, you're *Second* Director. I'm First, and I was in the first—"

"Yeah, I get the picture," said Kaz. "It might not be so simple. Maybe we've got it all wrong. Maybe there's nothing to your newspaper story."

Hamish shook his head with that know-it-all look on his face. Kaz had been finding that look increasingly irritating lately. In fact, she'd been finding Hamish irritating full stop.

"I'm sure this newspaper story will turn out to be an evil we'll have to beat eventually," he said.

"Oh, you're sure, are you?" snapped Kaz. "Well, *I'm* sure that none of us is even close to going into a Vidz, so what do you make of that?"

"Who knows?" said Hamish.

"Who cares?" said Bo.

They both turned to stare at him.

"Like, stop fighting and all that," he continued. "Jeez. We've only just started being the Vidz crew, and you two are acting like you're brother and sister already. Ever thought that this might have nothing to do with us three? There's still a fourth Vidz director out there who we haven't met yet."

Hamish nodded. "Bo's right," he said. "It's silly to argue. We should just lie low and wait."

"Since when do you give the orders?" said Kaz.

"First Director, remember?" said Hamish.

"So?"

Hamish gave her one of his serene smiles, and Kaz exploded. "Don't smile at me like that," she said, smacking her dry lips. "I just don't get it. I mean, I understand the connection between the evil Lord Dudley and the evil toad Cushing. I just don't get this one. . . ."

"It'll work out," said Hamish.

"Stop sounding like you're some kind of expert all the time," snapped Kaz. "You're really annoying when you do that."

Her words came out hard and angry, and Kaz immediately regretted them. She hadn't meant to sound that way. In fact, she hadn't even meant to argue such a silly point for so long when she could be at home raiding the fridge. It was Hamish's fault, wasn't it? Or maybe it was Bolex and the hot day's fault. Or maybe her whole life was to blame. Hamish stared at her with a hurt expression on his face. Then he stood up and grabbed his bag.

"This discussion is useless," he said. "I'm going home."

"Hey, don't be like that, Hamish," said Bo.

Hamish shrugged, then walked away. Kaz sat down heavily, crossing her arms and staring darkly at nothing at all.

"What is wrong with you?" asked Bo, rubbing his disheveled hair. "You're like Frankenstein's bride at the moment."

"You would be too, if you were me," snapped Kaz.

"I would?"

"Yes. There's no way you could handle not having any money. It's horrible. I can't buy drinks. I can't do anything." Kaz had, by now, slipped completely into her misery. She stopped her litany when she saw the look of shock on Bo's face.

"Why didn't you just say something before?" said Bo. "I've got money. . . ."

"I'm sick of borrowing," said Kaz. "My life is so awful. I mean, what good is it being this amazing Vidz director when I can't even afford a few dollars for a cold drink? Sure, I can fight pus-ridden creatures, but don't ask me to have any fun in the real world."

"Jeez, Kaz," said Bo, picking up his bag and standing up. "It's only money."

Kaz looked at Bo's back as he made his way out of the canteen. Of course he was right. It *was* only money. She smiled at her old friend. They'd known each other since they were little kids. All through their lives they'd watched movies and wanted to be moviemakers. And then they both got into Capra Video High School, so they could learn about moviemaking every day. And as if that weren't enough, they had somehow both been chosen to fight evil inside the mysterious Vidz movies.

"Wait," said Kaz, running to join Bo as he walked out into the hot afternoon air. "You're right. My life is pretty incredible, really. I'll ring Hamish tonight and say sorry."

"Make sure you do, Kaz," said Bo, sounding serious for once in his life. "Hamish is okay, you know. He'd stick by you if you were in trouble."

"I know," said Kaz, feeling bad about how she'd treated him. "He's just always so . . . right."

"Hey, he *is* the First Director," said Bo. "Last time I looked at my Vidz DVD, it said Third Director, and yours said—"

"I know. Second Director." Kaz sighed. "So," she added, "when *was* the last time you looked at your Vidz?"

"Are you kidding?" laughed Bo. "I never stop looking at it."

"There's going to be another Vidz movie, isn't there, Bo? I mean, it's not all over, is it?"

"No way," said Bo, crossing the road at the lights. "It's only just begun."

Kaz could feel the heat rising from the bitumen. Luckily her house was air-conditioned. She'd go home, put her feet up, and watch a movie. One of the good things about going to a video high school was that you could claim watching vids as part of your homework. The teachers even *encouraged* you to do it.

"What I need," said Kaz as they passed the shops, "is one of those time-travel movies. You know, the ones where kids go back in time and change something about the past to fix their problems."

"What would you change?" asked Bo.

"Well, I'd go back and stop Cushing from swindling my dad and making him go broke."

"Yeah," said Bo, thinking deeply. "But I've seen those time-travel movies. It's never as easy as that."

"It wouldn't be that hard to stop Cushing. . . ."

"No, I mean, like, you change the past and sometimes you change stuff you didn't want to change. Like, Cushing came to Capra High after he robbed your dad. So, you stop him in reel one of your time-travel movie, wouldn't that mean that Cushing didn't come to work at Capra High in reel two?"

"I dunno." Kaz shrugged. "Who cares?"

"Not me," said Bo.

They dodged the hot mothers with prams and the sweltering pedestrians with too much shopping. Let the evil sweat it out in the heat, they were going home to cool off.

2
Scene two

Meanwhile, somewhere near Capra Video High School, evil *was* at work . . . but in a cool, dark place.

A boy spends the afternoon at the cinema.

An innocent pastime . . .

. . . until an evil flickering begins.

Another teenager falls
into the trap.

3

Scene three

Kaz woke the next morning in an even grumpier mood than the day before. The house was stuffy and hot, and she'd slept badly from sweating and tossing all night. She stumbled into the bathroom to splash cold water on her face, passing the air-conditioner switch on the way through. It would be so easy to turn it on and get some cold air flowing through the house, but her father had said the day before that they couldn't afford the extra electricity. Kaz had totally lost it when he told her that.

"You're kidding!" she'd yelled. "I've just had a horrible, hot day. I want to cool off!"

"It costs way too much, Kaz," her father had said.

An awful look crossed his face then, a mix of sadness and panic. It had given Kaz a jolt seeing it, and she wanted to tell her dad that everything would be okay, but she couldn't do it. This was her father, who had always been so strong and confident and successful. What could she say? In the end, he'd beaten her to it.

"There's going to be a few other luxuries we'll have to do without," he'd said, a note of warning in his voice.

"Like what?" Kaz had said.

"Like a *lot*," he'd said. "You'll have to prepare. . . ."

But Kaz had stopped listening. All her soft feelings for her dad evaporated in the hot, stifling air around her. "It's like living in a prison around here," she'd said. "Ever since the business went broke. I hate my life, and I *hate* this family!"

She'd stormed to her room and slammed the door, only to sneak out later to the TV room and watch a movie. Her mum had stuck her head round the door and said dinner was ready, but Kaz had refused to eat.

"Maybe you'll save a few dollars," she'd snapped, regretting her comment later.

It wasn't her mum's fault, it was her dad's. Why did he have to trust Cushing? Why did he have to lose so much money? And why did he have to overreact? All this nagging over a few little things like air-conditioning was silly. They weren't *that* broke, were they? They still had their nice furniture, and the TV and home theater setup. Not to mention their lovely house. Surely they could afford a bit of cool air now and then?

Kaz had a cold shower, then dressed, feeling hot by

the time she'd done up her shoelaces. At least some of the rooms at school would be air-conditioned. She went into the kitchen and was sitting down to her breakfast when she heard strange deep voices in the house. There were men in the TV room. Kaz went to the door and looked down the hallway to see two large fellows dressed in T-shirts and shorts carrying the TV out of the house.

"Hey!" she shouted. "What's going on?"

"Ask your dad, sweetheart," mumbled one of the men.

Kaz walked down to the TV room, her father's warning from last night replaying in her head. She bumped into him in the hall.

"There you are," he said. "I wanted to talk with—"

"Where are they taking *my* TV?" demanded Kaz.

"Now, calm down. . . ."

"Dad!"

"We can't afford it, love. The TV, the home theater. It's like I said, we'll have to do without a few luxuries for a while. . . ."

Kaz stared at her father in disbelief. What was he talking about? How *dare* he allow them to take away the TV? Next they'd be taking the DVD player. . . . A cold, horrible shiver trickled down Kaz's spine, and she ran into the TV room to see a gaping hole where the DVD player had once sat.

"No!" she shouted, running back out to her father. "Dad! What are you doing? You can't take the DVD player away. I need it!"

"I know, love. And believe me, it was a hard decision, but there's always the library at school to watch your videos."

"The *what*?" shrieked Kaz. "You don't understand, I *have* to have the DVD player. I might be the next . . . I mean . . . oh, forget it!"

She ran to her room. At least she still had a DVD player in her computer. She could use that to watch the Vidz movie, if and when she was called upon. But the scene in her room was even more disastrous than in the TV room. Another man was bundling her computer into a cardboard box.

"That's my computer!" shouted Kaz.

"I'm afraid not, kid. This computer belongs to the store. It was only leased, up until yesterday, that is. But don't worry. They back everything up onto a CD before they wipe the hard drive. Your information is safe and confidential."

"Who cares about the information!" shouted Kaz. "I need that DVD player."

The man grinned at her, then picked up the computer box effortlessly. "You'll live without your videos for a while, I reckon." He walked past her and out of the room.

"It's more than just videos," said Kaz feebly, flopping heavily onto the bed.

She stared at the empty desk for a while, until tears started flowing down her cheeks. This was the worst nightmare imaginable. She was nobody now. No longer popular Kaz or rich Kaz, and most importantly, she was no longer Vidz Kaz. They'd have to throw her out of the Vidz crew. How could she stay without her own DVD player? And she hadn't had the chance to star in her own Vidz. She'd just been a bit player in Hamish's.

Kaz allowed her misery to build to a crescendo, not bothering to look up when her father came to her door.

"Sorry, love," he said.

Kaz didn't move. If she'd looked, she would have seen that he had a sad expression on his face, and that his whole body seemed slumped and smaller than usual. Instead, she turned her head away, staring angrily at the wall. Right now her dad was the last person in the world she wanted to talk to. He'd ruined her life, and all because he was too soft and trusting.

"Look, Kaz," said her father. "It won't be forever."

"Leave me alone."

"As soon as I'm back on my feet, we'll get an even bigger TV. . . ."

Kaz swung around, tears in her eyes, and shouted at the top of her voice, "I said leave me alone! You've wrecked everything. Can't you even see that? Everything."

She swept all her DVDs off the shelf onto the floor, then kicked at them. The Vidz skittled across to her father, and he bent to pick it up, his face grim and dark.

"It will get better," he said in a small voice.

Kaz grabbed her school bag, then swept past her father, snatching the Vidz from him on the way through.

"You've got no idea," she said.

4

Scene four

And in another bedroom, not far from Kaz's home, a different drama was being played out.

Another burglary.

"Jason! What are you doing with my purse?"

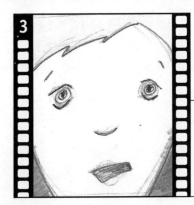

"Don't panic. I'm not here to hurt you."

"Jason? Why are you talking like that? I'm your mother. . . ."

5

Scene five

The cool blast of the school library atmosphere was such a relief that Kaz breathed a sigh. She stood at the entrance looking at the rows upon rows of DVDs and old VHS tapes before her. Old black-and-white movies, recent Hollywood movies, Indian, French, German, Spanish movies . . . they were *all* here. There were books in this library as well, but nowhere near the same number as movies.

It was nearly half an hour before school started, and hardly anyone was around. One of the senior students who assisted in the library was behind the desk.

"Where's Mrs. Leigh?" asked Kaz.

Mrs. Leigh was the school librarian, a friendly, flamboyant woman with film-star looks—long blond hair, tanned skin, and a young face. She was new to the school, and had the most amazing number of facts about films and film history stored in her head. The students were always coming to her with questions.

"She'll be in soon," said the senior student.

"Oh," said Kaz. "It's just that I asked her to check out some videos for me. . . ."

"And you are?"

"Kaz Murneau."

"I'll have a look for you."

The student went into the office, and Kaz leant against the counter. She'd come to the librarian asking for a list of movies that had women in the bad guy role. It was after one of the many arguments she'd had with Hamish. He was talking about the bad guys they might face in a Vidz, and Kaz had said, "Hang on. What if the bad guy is female?"

Hamish had given her one of his superior looks, and said bad guy was just a phrase, and it included men and women. Kaz had laughed and said why didn't he refer to bad gals as well? Then he'd said that it was probably because all the *really good* bad roles went to men. Then he listed roles like evil cops, corrupt politicians, bullies at school, dark lords, and mad wizards, until Kaz's head started to spin. She wanted to interject and throw in some evil women roles, but in truth, she didn't know any. How could she outdo Hamish? His knowledge of film history was huge. Probably the only

person in the school who knew more than he did was
Mrs. Leigh.

Kaz started to grow impatient. It didn't matter now
about bad guys or women. In fact, nothing seemed
important anymore. Her life was totally slipping away.
She knew it wasn't Hamish she was really angry with. He
didn't lose all her family's money.

The senior student finally returned from the office,
shaking his head. "There's nothing there," he said. "What
were you after?"

"It was just stuff about evil women in movies. You
know, bad gals . . ."

"Femme fatales," said the senior.

"Femme what?"

"It's French. Fatal woman, or something like that.
They were always gorgeous, and it was like you never
knew if they were a victim or a smart operator. In the old
black-and-white movies."

"So when did you find out if they were, like, *bad*,
then?"

"Usually in the last reel of the movie. We've got
heaps of these movies, film noirs, complex and moody.
Not like today's films, which are so simple with their
good guys and bad guys. Check out the old Bette Davis
movies. Or Joan Crawford in *Mildred Pierce* . . ."

Kaz started to giggle. The senior was off on his own
little movie history lecture, just like Hamish.

"What?" he said.

"Nothing . . . sorry. I think I just lost an argument.
But . . . hey!" A thought came to her. "Got any movies
about time travel?"

"Heaps," said the student. "There's the *Back to the Future* series. There's all the versions of H. G. Wells's *The Time Machine*, there's—"

"Okay," said Kaz, grinning. "Just one will do."

"Sure thing," said the student, going over to the video shelves. "We have a DVD right here. . . ."

"Oh," said Kaz. "Um . . . my DVD player broke down."

"Watch it in the viewing room. What you don't finish now you can watch after school."

Kaz smiled, remembering her dad had suggested the same thing. Why not? Maybe she had overreacted this morning. She signed for the DVD, then walked past a lone girl sitting near the viewing room. The girl was in Kaz's year, and she had the wildest silver nail polish on. She gave a shy smile, and Kaz said a quick hello, wondering what her name was before shutting the door to the tiny room behind her. She sat down at the desk and turned on the DVD player, removing the disk from its case. When Kaz leant over to put it into the machine, her bag fell from her lap. The Vidz tumbled out to lie at her feet. Kaz picked it up and gasped. It was heavier than usual. She dropped the school's disk and opened the case to the Vidz. The DVD inside was warm. Kaz felt the Vidz case, but it was cool.

"Whoa," she whispered.

Was this it? She looked at the Vidz, her hand shaking a little. *I should get Hamish,* she thought. But she quickly rejected that idea. She could handle this. After all, she'd been in Hamish's Vidz, even if it was a minor part. Taking a deep breath, Kaz inserted the Vidz DVD into the machine.

Please let this be it, she thought.

The TV screen flickered, then the words *Second Director* appeared in white. They slowly changed to *Vidz.*

"Yes!" whispered Kaz. "Here goes. . . ."

The screen went black for a second or two; then sad music started playing. An image started to form, a close-up of a child's toy. The camera moved from the toy, passing over another toy, then a teddy, then to some pictures on a shelf. It was tracking around a child's room, showing all of her possessions, all of her life, her history. There were photographs of a young girl laughing on a swing, then of the same girl slightly older, riding a bicycle. Now she was in a school uniform with braces on her teeth. The camera stopped at a final photograph of the girl looking out from the frame, a sad, confused expression on her face. Her face seemed familiar. Next a title faded up over the photograph: *Time Trap.*

"Time trap," whispered Kaz.

The music stopped; then a strange throbbing started in Kaz's temples. Her vision grew blurry and dim.

"Okay. Okay. I can deal with this," said Kaz, trying to squash her panic.

All she could see was a fuzzy light coming from the TV screen, growing larger and larger, as if the TV were moving toward her.

I'm falling into it, thought Kaz. *And now there'll be that weird kind of voice thingy. . . .*

A faraway sound rang in her ears. It was the voice, emitting one long, loud call. "Aaaaaaaaaaa . . ." Forming into words. "Aaaaaand action!" Without warning, the light hurtled toward her at great speed, and Kaz let out a cry. A branch or a bush smacked her in the face; then she landed on her backside on some grass.

She was in the Vidz.

6

Scene six

Kaz sat in the middle of a park, or maybe it was a small town square. There were roads all the way round its perimeter, and benches neatly laid out around a trimmed rose garden. *This looks like one of those small American towns you see in the movies,* she thought. The square was packed with people, and stalls had been set up selling cold drinks, confectionery, and cakes. Obviously some kind of fair or celebration was going on.

Kaz stood slowly, brushing herself down. What had she been doing? *I have to keep running. . . .* She shook her head. Where had that come from? Why did she have to keep running? She'd only just landed. She knew from Hamish that she'd feel strong urges that wouldn't necessarily make sense at first. This came from the Vidz, from being the character in the movie. Whatever was happening to that character, whatever she felt, Kaz would now feel too.

Just wish I knew where I'm supposed to run to.

A rotunda stood to one side of the square, and the town band were tuning their instruments inside. Near the rotunda was what looked to be a large statue of a man and a woman. People were milling around it. Kaz looked at the statue and felt a pang of sadness fill her body. She remembered the titles sequence to this Vidz. It had been rather sad. Maybe this movie was a tearjerker.

No sword fighting for me, then.

She turned to see that she was next to a row of sideshow attractions. A series of trick mirrors showed her reflection in distorted shapes. Kaz walked up to one of the mirrors that was normal and looked at herself. Her Vidz face was the same age as in real life, but more serious, and sadder. Her hair was longer, pulled back in a conservative style, but she was still Kaz. It was so strange, looking at herself as a character in a movie. Memories came to her as she stared at her face. She remembered a childhood. She'd been taught at home. Not many friends to play with. What was she? A young genius. Yes, there was no mathematical problem she couldn't solve. There was a brilliant woman in her memory too, and Kaz had a warm feeling thinking about her. *She helped me with something important . . . an experiment . . .*

A voice in the background started nagging at Kaz's brain. It was calling the same name over and over.

"Kathleen. Kathleen."

Kathleen? Who the heck is that?

Kaz turned to see a policeman in the distance, wearing one of those blue uniforms cops wear in the American movies. He was smiling straight at her.

Could I be Kathleen?

"That's the way, Kathleen. We'll have a little talk, then. . . ."

The policeman had an Irish American accent. His voice sounded friendly enough, but there was something about his smile that gave Kaz a warning. It was too frozen, too forced. She'd had the urge to run before, and now this cop was coming for her. There was no time to stop and work out whose side he was on. She had to go with her instinct.

Kaz turned and ran toward the busiest part of the square. She figured that it would be easier to hide in among the crowd than out on the streets. There was a large tent set up in the middle of the square, and most of its flaps were closed. Kaz saw a small opening and squeezed into the tent. It was dark inside, a perfect hiding place. Rows of people were sitting watching a movie that was being projected onto a portable screen. Kaz took a seat in the dimmest part of the tent and ducked her head low. She looked over her shoulder at the flap. The cop poked his head through, squinting in the darkness.

Kaz quickly turned back to the screen, then kept herself as still as possible so that she wouldn't stand out in the dark. The movie flickered before her, some documentary about two famous scientists. There were shots of them in their laboratory, doing experiments. Now the voice-over was talking about a famous discovery that the scientists had made. Kaz felt a tight knot grow in her throat.

I know them. . . .

The voice-over named the scientists: Maryanne and Thomas O'Bride. There was a shot of the two scientists with their children. Two delightful little girls, one dark and the other fair. The dark girl had a brooding look about her, as if she was a bit angry with the world. The camera showed a close-up of the dark sister, and Kaz felt a tear trickle down her cheek.

That girl . . . that's . . . me.

The slow realization hit her. This was a shot of herself when she was young. No! It was a shot of her Vidz self. . . . *But it feels like it's me.* Kathleen O'Bride. Daughter of the famous O'Brides. The narrator's voice-over in the movie told the story. The O'Brides' fame came from finding a cure to Miller's Syndrome, a deadly disease that had slowly been killing children all over the world, especially in developing nations. Her Vidz parents were heroes. They were saints.

They're dead.

Kaz knew this in her heart, in her soul. She knew it just as she knew every little detail of her real family life back at Capra. Her Vidz parents were dead, and that statue near the rotunda was of them. That's what this whole day was about, a day to celebrate her famous parents.

So why is there a policeman out there chasing me? What have I done wrong?

The documentary looked as if it was coming to an end, and Kaz decided to get out of there before they opened the flaps and she was stuck inside. She crept along the ground toward the front and found another flap that was held closed by a chair. Removing the chair carefully, Kaz poked her head outside. The sunlight blinded her for a second, but when her eyes had adjusted she saw no sign of the cop. The band were still practicing in the rotunda.

A small tent stood next to the rotunda, with a sign tacked carelessly over its entrance: YOUR FORTUNE TOLD! Sitting at a table outside the tent was an older woman dressed in an outrageous fortune-teller's costume, complete with a purple turban. She had an upturned fishbowl on the table and was clutching a man's hand, looking intently into his eyes.

That'd be the fortune-teller, then, thought Kaz. *Could I hide there?*

Just then the woman looked up and met Kaz's eyes across the square. An instant feeling of warmth and safety filled Kaz's heart. Now she knew where she had to go.

Kaz slipped through the flap and made a dash for the fortune-teller's tent. The woman winked at her as she ran by. Kaz ducked inside the little tent, wondering exactly what the future held for her in this Vidz. As soon as her eyes adjusted to the gloom in the tent, she saw a girl, slightly younger than Kaz, with long blond hair severely pulled back and a pretty summer dress on. She wore thick glasses and had pale pink nail polish on her fingernails that clashed with her dress. Kaz took all this in, settling on the girl's nervous face. There was something familiar about her, but Kaz knew that she would meet characters in the Vidz who she thought she knew.

"Kaz?" said the girl the minute she entered the tent.

"You know my name?" said Kaz.

Whoa! Listen to me. I've got an American accent, just like this girl.

"Yes, I know your name," said the girl, a wary look on her face. Then she laughed nervously and said, "I should . . . I'm your sister."

"But . . . I mean, aren't I Kathleen?"

"Is this a trick question?" asked the girl. "Because, you know, Kathleen . . . Kaz. It's just a short version."

Kaz waved her hand at the girl. "Sorry," she said. "I guess I was . . . was . . ." *I was what? You're my sister? So I should know you. Your name is . . . Abigail.* "Sorry, Abigail. God . . . everything is so weird. There's a cop out there. . . . He chased me."

"What did he say?"

"Nothing. That he wanted to talk . . ."

Abigail went to the opening and looked outside, coming back with a worried look on her face.

"Do you think he knows?" she said. "Do you think he's trying to stop us?"

Kaz did her best to look thoughtful. *I'd answer your question, sis, if I actually knew what it was we are going to do.* She hoped they weren't planning to rob a bank or something revolting like that. Abigail was still waiting for an answer to her question, so Kaz shrugged. "Who knows?" she said. "Everything has gone strange. . . ."

"I'm scared," said Abigail, a haunted look on her face. Then she stared closely at her big sister, searching Kaz's face for something. An answer, perhaps, or comfort? Eventually she whispered, "Do you know why?"

Kaz panicked. She felt for a brief moment that this Abigail was testing her somehow, but that was ridiculous. *I'm just being paranoid.* None of the characters in Hamish's Vidz had tested him; as far as they had been concerned, he was the real deal. Since she had no idea why her sister would be scared, Kaz decided to just play the role of the bossy big sister.

"Snap out of it," she said, sounding a little too hard and mean. "We haven't got time for you to be scared."

To her relief, Abigail did snap out of her frightened state, adopting a cold, superior expression instead.

"Fine," she said. "Sorry I even spoke. In fact, sorry I even exist in the first place. . . ."

Kaz rolled her eyes. Was she going to have to deal with this little sister *all* through the movie? In her real life she was an only child and didn't have to bother with the complications siblings brought. "Listen, let's get a few things straight," she said. "Whatever is about to happen, just don't get in my way. Okay?"

"I suppose you're in charge, are you?" said Abigail with a sneer.

"As a matter of fact, I am."

I am? How come I am? Hey . . . I'm Big Sister. I'm number . . .

"I'm number one," said Kaz. "Got it? What I say goes."

"What about Mrs. Bates?"

Kaz was about to say "Mrs. who?" when the image

of the outrageous fortune-teller came to her. That had to be Mrs. Bates. So, what about her? She was in on what they were about to do. *In fact, she encouraged me, made me feel special . . . proud . . .*

"Don't you think she might want to have a say too?" said Abigail. "After all, you and her built it together. . . ."

Built it? Built what?

"You did bring it with you, didn't you?" said Abigail.

For the first time since she'd entered the Vidz, Kaz realized that she was wearing a backpack. It suddenly felt heavy, and she slung it from her shoulders, letting it sit gently on the ground.

"Yes," she said. "I brought it. It's in here."

Kaz unzipped her pack and pulled out a small box with two golden dials on the front. One dial was labeled DAYS, the other HOURS. The box had two small gold-plated arms that stood up at an angle. A fine carbon-based aerial was strung between them, and it shimmered in the dull interior of the tent with its own silvery gleam. The aerial was so fragile it quivered dramatically as Kaz moved the box around.

"Careful, *boss,*" warned Abigail, sneering and pointing to the aerial. "Don't want to snap it, do you?"

"No," said Kaz, stilling her hand. She concentrated on the box, wondering what the heck it was.

Hours. Days. Aerial . . . My gosh! Could it be?

"It's a time machine," whispered Kaz.

Abigail giggled beside her. "Of course it's a time machine, dummy. What do you think you've been making these past years? A TV remote?"

No, this was no remote. This was an amazing

invention, a powerful tool that could transport anyone back in time. The potential for doing good with a tool like this was enormous. Kaz felt her heart thumping with pride. *I made this. Me . . . Nobody believed I could do it. Not my parents, not my school . . . only Mrs. Bates. She believed.* Memories about Mrs. Bates flooded into Kaz's brain. She was a brilliant scientist who had worked for Kaz's parents. In fact, she was almost part of the family.

Kaz could see images, like flashbacks in a movie. Mrs. Bates at the dinner table with them, laughing, sharing a joke. Kaz saw her parents, stiff, remote. Her father lost in his thoughts, her mother talking only to *him* about work. Mrs. Bates had always been there, providing the lightness and cheer that every child needed.

Then something changed. There was an argument, a terrible yelling row between Mrs. Bates and Kaz's father. He banned her from the laboratory, and he banned her from the family! Dinnertime returned to being a cold, humorless affair, when they listened to their father drone on about Miller's Syndrome. Kaz and Abigail had missed their friend dreadfully.

Then she had returned to their lives, in secret, encouraging them, helping them, never having a harsh word for Kaz's father even after he'd treated her so badly. She was the one who had recognized the potential in Kaz's mathematical experiments. She was the one who had helped build this time machine. She was the one who had first told Kaz she was a genius.

"Not that Dad would ever have noticed," muttered Kaz.

"What'd you say?" said Abigail.

Kaz snapped out of her reverie and looked again

at the time machine. Here it was. Ready to transport them back in time. Ready to help them do what no human in history had ever done.

"This is incredible," whispered Kaz. "Let's use it now."

"Now?" said Abigail. "But what about Mrs. Bates?"

Kaz looked through the flap. Mrs. Bates still had a line of customers waiting to have their fortunes told. There was time enough to fiddle with time!

"Come on," she said, fingering the Days dial on the machine. "Just a little trip, eh?"

"No," said Abigail, shaking her head. "Mrs. Bates said—"

"Oh, Mrs. Bates, Mrs. Bates. Is she all you ever think about?"

"That's just so typical of you," hissed Abigail. "You are so self-centered! You always have to be the one, don't you? Everyone tiptoes around Kathleen because *she's* the genius. . . ."

Kaz was taken aback for a second. "Whoa!" she shouted, holding up her hand. There wasn't time for this debate, especially when it concerned a fictional character and not her real self. Let Abigail explode some other time.

"Look, I'm going to try this now, with or without you. So if you want to come for the ride, decide now."

"Oh, I *hate* you," said Abigail.

She clutched her older sister's arm, and Kaz spun the dial. They stared at the machine. Nothing happened. When would it work? She spun the dial a little more and waited. Still nothing.

Abigail gave her a know-it-all smile and said, "You could try putting the fuel in."

"The fuel? Oh . . . right. And the fuel is . . ."

"Stop playing stupid games. It's in your bag."

Kaz reached into the backpack and pulled out a novelty wristwatch with a cartoon character smiling out from the dial. She looked at the time machine and saw that there was a slot small enough to slide the watch into. It seemed like the most logical thing to do, so Kaz slid the watch in. She was about to say something to Abigail when her whole world blew apart.

Sucked away to another time . . .

The time travelers arrive in the park.

"Abigail! There!"

"Mum and Dad's statue. They put that up last week!"

"That must mean . . . ," whispered Kaz, staring at the statue as it was righted into position.

"That we traveled back in time," whispered Abigail. "Over a week. It worked!"

"I remember this day," said Kaz. "I felt kinda numb, and . . ."

She squeezed back the tears, remembering the awful emptiness of missing her parents. Of feeling alone. Of . . . *Wait a minute! I have parents. Two of them. Get a grip.*

Kaz watched as the statue was slowly settled onto its base. There was a small crowd around, but none of the faces seemed familiar. Except one. The policeman. He was standing well away from the group, almost behind a clump of bushes. Could he see them? No, the cop seemed to be distracted, talking to someone who had his or her back to them. *Who is that? I think it might be . . .*

Kaz was distracted by a sharp hiss from Abigail. "Kaz," she whispered, pointing to the small crowd around the base of the statue. Kaz had a closer look and gasped. There, at the front of the crowd, was herself. Or rather, herself a week ago.

"That is so weird," whispered Kaz. "I mean . . . that's me!"

"I think we should go," said Abigail.

"What if we met? Talked to each other?"

"No!" shouted Abigail. "You can't tamper with time. You know that. You go meet yourself a week ago, it could complicate everything. What if that Kaz over there started having nightmares about meeting herself? What if she never makes it to the fortune-telling tent because of the nightmares? What if you never got here because of that?"

"Okay, enough!" said Kaz, scratching her head. "I get it. Don't mess with the past."

"Let's go back now," said Abigail.

"Sure thing," said Kaz, turning the box over. "Now, to go back, all I have to do is . . . um . . ." She saw a button labeled NOW underneath the box. That would have to be it. The Now button would hopefully return them to the time when they left. With a shaking finger, Kaz pressed the button, and they were sucked into the time vortex again.

She landed softly back inside the fortune-telling tent and stared at the box in her hands. Such a simple, innocent-looking thing, yet it held tremendous power. Kaz thought of all the good that could be done with a time machine. History could be changed, tragedy stopped, wars finished before they started. This was a machine that could give the world so much love and happiness and peace . . .

And evil, thought Kaz.

It could also create evil.

7

Scene seven

EXT. CITY STREET, DAY

HAMISH and BO are walking down a city street, their schoolbags over their shoulders. There are run-down and dusty shops lining the footpath, and a few people walking by.

>BO
>So Kaz didn't ring you last night?

>HAMISH
>Nope.

BO

But, like, she said she would. Oh well, I'll ask her
about it when we get to school this morning.

HAMISH

What's with her lately? She's been so hard to live
with.

BO

Things are tough for her, you know, because of her
dad.

HAMISH

I'm worried about her, Bo. If she enters a Vidz with
this huge attitude problem, well, she might . . .

BO

Hey. Kaz is solid gold. She wouldn't do anything
wrong. Okay?

HAMISH

Okay.

They pass a small cinema with the name STAR CINEMA on the
outside. A woman is locking the door. She is MRS. LEIGH, the
school librarian. Mrs. Leigh seems very surprised to see them.

MRS. LEIGH

Good morning, boys. It's . . . now, don't tell me.
Harry and Ben, right?

Hamish and Bo stop.

BO

Actually, it's Hamish and Bo, Mrs. Leigh.

Hamish looks up at the sign above the cinema.

HAMISH

What are you doing here?

MRS. LEIGH

I could ask you two the same question. This
isn't the sort of area I'd expect to find Capra
kids. A bit more down-market than what
you're used to. I was just off to the school.
(She indicates the cinema behind her.)
This is my little business, boys. Didn't you
know I ran a cinema?

BO

That is so cool. Your own cinema. That is my
dream, man. Wow! What movies do you show?

MRS. LEIGH

Oh, strange, quirky little titles.

HAMISH

Maybe we should come along and see one. Have you
got a list?

Mrs. Leigh looks at them, distracted, as if she's thinking
about something else.

HAMISH
Mrs. Leigh?

MRS. LEIGH
Hm?

HAMISH
A list of the movies you're showing.

MRS. LEIGH
(laughs) Oh, you two boys don't want to come in
here. It's small and dirty. . . . No, this isn't the
cinema for you. There's much bigger and better
screens in town.

BO
Oh . . . but . . .

MRS. LEIGH
No, no, boys. You're a couple of nice lads. You stick
to homework and telling stories about your day at
the dinner table. This is a rough part of town. You
might get hurt hanging around here.

She laughs at some private joke.

>   HAMISH
>   Oh. Well . . . see you at school, I suppose.

>   MRS. LEIGH
>   Bye, boys. I'd offer you a lift, but regulations
>   . . . you understand.

She walks down the street in the opposite direction
from Hamish and Bo.

>   HAMISH
>   Was that just the weirdest conversation you've
>   ever heard or what?

>   BO
>   Hey, Mrs. Leigh is cool. She's seen so many
>   movies, and she helped me out heaps with
>   my film history essay. She's about the only
>   grown-up I know who I can talk to about
>   movies. I like her.

>   HAMISH
>   I just don't get it, that's all. She tells us she
>   shows movies, then she says we shouldn't
>   come in. It was like . . . like she didn't think
>   we were good enough for her. Or that we were
>   too good, or something. Maybe she's on
>   medication.

BO
(laughs)
Sure thing, Hamish. Man, you see bad guys
everywhere.

They walk off.

8

Scene eight

Mrs. Bates stood over the two girls, shaking her head as she looked at the cartoon watch in Kaz's hand.

"But I don't understand," she said. "That was a new watch. How can it be empty of fuel?"

"Beats me," lied Kaz.

Of course, she knew that the watch was empty of fuel, of time, because they'd used it all up going back a week to see the statue being put into place. Each watch was only good for two time trips, a fact that Kaz had taken great delight in not only knowing but also reminding her little sister of. Mrs. Bates placed her arm around Kaz's shoulder and asked, "Is there something you want to tell me?"

Kaz felt the warmth from the woman's touch. It was so familiar to her, so comforting. All this time she'd been missing her parents, hurting so much inside, and Mrs. Bates had been there for her like a solid rock. How could she lie to her? It felt so wrong. And yet . . . it felt wrong to reveal everything right now. A nagging thought came back to her that something didn't add up. Kaz shook her head to try and clear it away.

"I'm fine," she said.

Mrs. Bates smiled, her face glowing with pride for her special student. "This is it, Kathleen. All this time we worked together, when everyone tried to stop you. This is your glorious moment—history's glorious moment. Nobody believed you could do this. . . ."

Mrs. Bates' voice trailed off for a second, and Kaz could see the pain on her face. Yes, this woman had been hurt too, by the same people who'd hurt Kathleen. Maryanne and Thomas O'Bride. All they ever thought about was their work. It hadn't mattered to them that they'd ignored their children and trampled on Mrs. Bates in the process. Kaz felt a burning anger growing inside her. They were so selfish.

"Excuse me," said Abigail, her arms crossed. "Sorry to interrupt the Genius Society, but we still don't have a watch."

"I'll get one," said Kaz.

"But," said Abigail. "The pol—" She cut short her protest, warned by a look from her sister.

"You come, Abbey," said Kaz. "Run interference."

"Abbey?" said Abigail, joining Kaz at the entrance of the tent. "Since when do you call me Abbey?"

"Since now, I guess," said Kaz.

"Please hurry, Kathleen," said Mrs. Bates.

As soon as they were outside the tent, Abigail stopped her sister. "So, what was all the cloak-and-dagger stuff back there? Why couldn't we tell Mrs. Bates about the policeman looking for you?"

"I don't know," said Kaz. "I just . . . It seemed like a good idea at the time."

Abigail snorted, shaking her head. "Like going back in time to when our parents were alive? That still seem like a good idea too?"

Kaz stared at her sister. She hadn't mentioned this plan before, and yet . . . isn't that why she was here? Isn't that what Mrs. Bates had referred to back in the tent? This glorious moment in history? Kaz and Abigail were going to prevent her parents from dying. *Of course that's the plan. What else would I use a time machine for?* She remembered a conversation on a hot day. It was with a friend. . . . With Bo! *Who knows?* thought Kaz. *If I change the past in the Vidz . . . maybe the past will change in my own world. After all, whatever happens in a Vidz affects the world back at Capra.*

"It *is* a good idea, going back," said Kaz. "I miss Mum and Dad. Don't you?"

"Yes," snapped Abigail, a furious look on her face. "Of course I do. It just . . . it doesn't seem right. How can we change things like that? Make dead people live again?"

"They won't ever *be* dead," said Kaz. "Don't you get

it? We'll make sure they never catch that plane, that way they won't die." Kaz was amazed at how quickly her Vidz past came to her as she spoke. Up until now she hadn't been aware that her parents had died in a plane crash, but now she could see the newspaper headlines. Even see the photo of the wreckage of their light plane being lifted from the sea.

"Great," said Abigail, crossing her arms on her chest. "So Mum and Dad come back, and then I sit back and watch you three fight and argue all day long."

Kaz felt like exploding. What was Abigail's problem? "Don't be such a . . . a . . . little sister!" she said.

"Fine," said Abigail, stomping off in the opposite direction.

"And fine by me," said Kaz, walking as far away as she could. Why did the world need little sisters, anyway? She could do this on her own. Kaz scanned the stalls and saw what she was after. Not too far away was a sideshow stall where the punters had to throw a ball at a stack of cans to win a prize. Sure enough, on the top row was a brand-new novelty watch as a prize. She walked up to the stall, where a pimply boy was taking money and handing out the balls. Kaz pulled some coins from her pocket. The boy handed over the missiles.

As she lined up her shot, a voice whispered in her ear. "What are you doing?" It was Abigail.

"I'm going to knock over the cans and win a watch," said Kaz. "Do you think your feeble mind can cope with that?"

Abigail started laughing. "You? Kaz, you couldn't hit a cow if you were standing right in front of it."

"I couldn't?" said Kaz. That didn't seem right. Wasn't she a good throw? She had memories of playing sports, of shooting goals, but she couldn't be sure whose memories they were. "You've got the wrong gal, sister," said Kaz confidently. "Watch this cow go down."

She wound back her throwing arm and let fly with a shot that flipped out the side of her hand and hit the boy on the nose.

"Oi!" he shouted. "Watch it."

"Moo," said Abigail dryly. Then she smirked at her sister. "How could I have doubted you?"

"Here," said Kaz, handing over the last two balls. "You do it."

Abigail lined up her shot and sent all but one of the cans skittling.

"Lucky shot," muttered Kaz.

She watched as her sister lined up the remaining can. Accuracy was called for, and Abigail spent a good ten seconds balancing herself for the shot. She let fly with her throw just as a meaty hand landed on Kaz's shoulder.

"Kathleen," came the lilting voice of the persistent police officer.

Kaz watched the can fly from the shelf, then turned and kicked the cop in the shin. It was something she'd seen done in a thousand movies, but instead of hopping about in agony, the policeman just grinned as Kaz's foot bounced off his shinbone ineffectually.

"Ow! Ow!" cried Kaz. "I think I broke my toe."

"Come on, Kathleen, enough of the dramatics. You'd better be coming along. I've discovered a few things since our last chat."

Yeah, like how to arrest innocent girls! Kaz twisted out of the policeman's grasp, shouting, "Get the watch!" to her sister. Then she ran. Was this all she was going to do in this movie? Run away? Escape? Surely she could stop and fight? That was what Hamish got to do in his Vidz.

A couple of kids walked by with large, blow-up plastic hammers in their hands, and Kaz grabbed one, turning to face the policeman.

"Come on," she called. "I challenge you to a duel."

"What?" laughed the cop. "A duel of plastic hammers?"

"Better than swords," said Kaz.

The policeman grabbed the other plastic hammer and shaped up against Kaz, his feet nicely planted at hip width, his balance solid and buoyant. Kaz groaned. Trust her to challenge some kind of expert. Maybe this cop spent his spare time bashing his colleagues over the head with blow-up toys. He wasn't going to be an easy opponent.

Kaz stepped in to strike a blow, but the policeman sidestepped, then brought his hammer down onto her head. It bounced off with a resounding *thwop!*, and she staggered for a moment.

"Now will you listen to sense?" said the cop, relishing his mini-victory with a grin to the crowd.

Kaz took this opportunity to step in and push her hammer into his face. It squashed up against his mouth and nose, causing him to stumble backward.

"I cmph brpth!" he shouted, stepping back farther until he tripped over a cart, landing in the middle of a pyramid of sticky toffee apples. The cop sat up, toffee apples poking out from his head. He looked like a demented porcupine.

"Aaarrgh!" he cried.

Kaz danced on the spot, shaking her hammer above her head. She'd won! She'd won! Now she could go back and tell Hamish how she'd been a hero too! Maybe she should go in and bop the policeman on his head, see how he liked it. She was about to move when a hand grabbed her by the shirt.

Kaz turned to see Abigail with the watch. "Tick, tock," she said.

"Oh, right," said Kaz. She had more important things to do than turn policemen into porcupines. There were a mother and father to save from a light plane crash, and a family to repair.

The word *family* stayed in her mind as they ran to the fortune-telling tent. The way forward was so clear now. Nothing else mattered.

Scene nine

EXT. CITY STREET, DAY

HAMISH and BO are walking down a different street.
They stop at a house. Bo looks at his watch.

> BO
> You sure this won't take long? School's gonna
> start any minute.

> HAMISH
> It's okay. Kaz can cover for us if we're late.
> This is where one of those kids lived. Jason.

BO
What did Jason steal?

HAMISH
Not much. His mum caught him in the act and
rang the police straightaway.

BO
Rang the police straightaway? Wow! Now that's
a loving mum for you.

The next-door neighbor comes down to her fence and
stares at them. Both Hamish and Bo squirm a little.

HAMISH
Um . . . hi.

NEIGHBOR
What do you two want? More criminals, are
ya?

HAMISH
Criminals?

NEIGHBOR
Like that little brat Jason.

BO
He was just a kid. He wasn't, like, a criminal.

NEIGHBOR

No? Then how come he's in custody, eh? That's where criminals wind up. I told his mother, I told her, you put that boy away. He has an evil look about him. . . .

Hamish and Bo now stare at the woman, wondering at the vitriol in her voice.

HAMISH

His mother locked him away?

NEIGHBOR

(laughs)

Best thing she ever did. Little brat was always arguing with her. It was World War Three in there.

BO

But . . . he was her son. I mean . . .

The woman moves closer, giving Bo a close inspection.

NEIGHBOR

I don't like the look of you, son. You're definitely another criminal. I think I might call the police. . . .

HAMISH

Hey, no need for that. We were just on our way.

NEIGHBOR
Well, you'd better run before I change my
mind. Go on . . . run!

BO
Okay, we're going!

Hamish and Bo hurry from the house.

BO
Friendly neighborhood.

HAMISH
Imagine calling the cops on your own kid.

BO
Yeah, man. Doesn't sound like that mother
understood old Jason any better than that old
bat did. . . .

HAMISH
He must have been one unhappy guy.

BO
You can say that again. But not as unhappy as
the new bursar's gonna be when we arrive at
school. We're, like, molto late.

They start running.

10

Scene ten

As they ran around a corner, the fortune-telling tent in sight, Abigail suddenly grabbed Kaz by the arm and pulled her behind a stall. They stood there panting, hoping the cop didn't see them.

"This is all too neat," said Abigail, catching her breath.

"Huh?"

"Come on, you felt it too. Before, when you had a nagging doubt, that's why you didn't tell Mrs. Bates about the cop."

"No," said Kaz. "It wasn't that. It was . . . um . . ."

"Why would Mrs. Bates help us bring Mum and Dad back?" said Abigail. "Why help you build a time machine and not claim credit? Why suggest we save our parents in the first place? They were disgusting to her. They threw her out over some . . . some . . . something." Abigail paused, a confused expression on her face. Obviously she couldn't remember what had started the rift between her parents and their ex-assistant.

It seemed curious to Kaz that Abigail couldn't remember. She tried to rack her own brain to remember what had caused the argument between Mrs. Bates and her father, but she came up with a blank too.

"And look at us," continued Abigail. "I mean . . . we had a horrible life with Mum and Dad. And here we are, trying to bring them back again."

Abigail laughed. Kaz laughed too. Now that she thought about it that way, it did seem absurd. She was going to bring back two cold, distant parents who hardly noticed she existed. Kaz sat on her haunches. Abigail followed.

"Do you remember much about Mum and Dad?" asked Kaz.

"A little," said Abigail, that nervous expression returning to her face. "Why?"

"I don't know," said Kaz. "All my memories are unhappy. It's like they never cared about us. . . . Families are weird."

"Let's not do this," whispered Abigail.

Kaz looked at Abigail and shook her head. "I have to," she said.

"Why?"

Why? That's a good question. She saw herself in another place, with friends, talking about evil . . . about something called Vidz.

"Because I've got to beat the bad guy," she said, knowing it sounded fairly crazy.

"Oh?" said Abigail. "And exactly who is the bad guy?"

Kaz froze. Abigail's question was like a slap to the face. She had no idea who the bad guy was. In fact, she'd almost forgotten that this was a Vidz. How could she let the character of Kathleen take over so completely? She had a job to do. Beat the bad guy. *But who* is *the bad guy?* There was no evil dark lord here. No obvious candidate. All she had was two dead parents and Mrs. Bates. *Could it be Mrs. Bates? No. That can't be right. I like her . . . no, I love her as if she were my mother.*

Maybe Abigail was right. Maybe they shouldn't go back in time just yet, until she worked out who she was supposed to defeat. Kaz was about to say this when a pair of large feet came into her vision.

"Now, now, no more antics, Kathleen," came the policeman's voice. "This time I have backup."

They were surrounded by a team of cops. Everywhere Kaz looked were blue legs and polished shoes. There was nowhere to run, nowhere to hide. A word came to her, and she knew she had to yell it and yell it loud.

"Cut!" she yelled at the top of her voice. "Cut!"

11

Scene eleven

The minute she returned to the library at Capra High, Kaz ran to get Hamish and Bo. She needed their help to figure out this Vidz. The hardest part was trying to stay Kaz and not let the character of Kathleen take over. Being the genius child muddled everything up. As she dashed out of the viewing room, a strange voice called out to her, "Kaz?", but she ignored it.

Leave me alone, she thought. *I don't have time to be popular.*

Kaz ran to the outside tables where she and Hamish and Bo usually hung out before school, but they weren't to be seen. None of the other students had clapped eyes on them that morning, either. The bell would sound any minute now, so Kaz headed for their first classroom, thinking they must have gone in early. That was empty too. She trudged back to the library, cursing them for not being around when she needed them most. Mrs. Leigh was entering the library as Kaz arrived, and she smiled, saying, "Good morning, Kaz."

"Oh, hi," said Kaz.

"Everything all right?"

"Hm? Um . . . yes, sort of."

"Now, why am I not convinced?" said Mrs. Leigh, putting her bag behind the library counter. She came over to Kaz and sat on a tabletop beside her. "You look like a heroine in trouble to me. Being chased, are you? Or are you chasing down the bad guys?"

"Hmph," said Kaz. "I wish I was."

"Oh, a cryptic answer," said Mrs. Leigh, smiling at her. "I like cryptic answers."

Kaz sat in a chair, relaxing a little. She liked Mrs. Leigh a lot. There weren't too many adults she could talk to like this. Maybe the librarian could help? Of course, Kaz couldn't reveal anything about Vidz to her, but maybe she could talk in an indirect way.

"There's this movie that I'm . . . er . . . studying," said Kaz.

"Title?"

"Oh, um . . . *Time Trap*."

"Never heard of it," said Mrs. Leigh.

"It's new," said Kaz. "Anyway . . . I've kind of seen the first half, and I'm trying to work out who the bad guy is. . . . There's this time machine, and two scientists who are my . . . *the* parents. And maybe it's one of them, or maybe I haven't met the bad guy. . . ." Kaz stopped, realizing that she was rambling on, *and* in danger of giving the Vidz secret away.

Mrs. Leigh straightened out the crease in her pants, deep in thought. "It sounds pretty complicated to me." Then she paused, looking at Kaz, before saying, "Everything all right at home, dear?"

To her embarrassment, Kaz started crying. The stress of the Vidz, on top of the horrible morning at home, all came crashing down on her. Mrs. Leigh put an arm around Kaz's shoulder and held her tight. After a moment or two she offered Kaz a tissue.

"Whenever my students start talking to me about obscure movies," she said, "I know it's code for troubles at home. Anything you want to talk about?"

Kaz shook her head, relieved that Mrs. Leigh hadn't twigged on to the Vidz. Let her think the *Time Trap* movie was code for home problems.

"Do you know," said Mrs. Leigh, "you should come to my cinema sometime. . . ."

"You own a cinema?"

"Just a small one. Called the Star. Come by and see a movie on the house. Cheer you up a little. We even have movies with bad guys in them. . . ."

Kaz laughed. "What about bad women?"

"Not too many of those, I'm afraid."

"But . . . your senior student. He said there were heaps. What'd he call them? Femme something."

Mrs. Leigh snorted, her face slightly red. 'What

would he know? Boys! They think the femme fatale roles were strong, but they weren't really. Those women mostly got the men to do their dirty work. No, what we gals need are really strong roles, where we can shake some muscle and show them who's the boss."

"I like the sound of that," said Kaz, wiping her eyes.

Mrs. Leigh looked off into the distance, an inspired expression on her face. "The true test, you know, will be when women can have both sorts of roles. Truly bad characters, nasty, evil—"

"And good characters, too," said Kaz. "Being the heroines."

"Oh yes," said Mrs. Leigh, smiling. "Absolutely." She looked at her watch. "Bell's about to sound. Better get to class."

"Okay," said Kaz. She paused. "I like what you said about girls taking charge. It's helped me, actually."

"It has? That's good," said Mrs. Leigh. She went behind the counter.

Kaz walked to the viewing room with a spring in her step. That's exactly what she'd do, take charge. She shut the door behind her, then made sure her Vidz was still in the DVD player. Satisfied that it was ready to go, Kaz pressed Play. She had some work to do.

12

Scene twelve

Back in the town square, and the press of police officers moved in on Kaz the instant she returned to the Vidz. It was as if no time had passed. The movie had moved seamlessly from one frame to the next. Except the Kaz in the last frame had panicked and yelled "Cut!" and the Kaz in this frame had worked out a plan. She grabbed Abigail by the hand and wound back the dial on the time machine five minutes. In a flash the policemen vanished.

"Great work," said Abigail. "Only you used up the watch again."

"No problem," said Kaz. She marched up to the stall where she'd won the watch, jumped the counter, and grabbed another watch, ignoring the protest of the pimply boy.

"Here," said Kaz, tossing him some money. "This'll buy ten of the things."

Then she and Abigail ran into the tent where Mrs. Bates waited.

"That was quick," said Mrs. Bates. "You've only been gone a minute or two."

"Well, time flies around here," said Kaz, removing the used watch from the time machine. "We're ready to go."

Mrs. Bates took a step forward and held Kaz's face, looking into her eyes. "How do you feel?" she asked softly.

"Scared," said Kaz.

Mrs. Bates nodded. "You can do this, Kaz. I believe in you. . . ."

Abigail coughed loudly and Mrs. Bates turned to her.

"And you, too, Abigail."

"Gee, thanks."

The woman stepped back and surveyed the two pioneer sisters. "Make sure you stop your mother and father from getting to that island. That's how you'll save them," she said.

Kaz wound back the dials on the time machine, then paused. Abigail's questions came back to her. Why was Mrs. Bates helping with the time machine, and with getting their parents back? She wanted to push the questions away, but the doubt just grew and grew. *Too neat.* That's what Abbey had said, and try as she might to ignore it, Kaz had to agree. It *did* feel too neat.

She looked at her mentor, her closest friend for the past few months, then took a deep breath. 'Can I ask you something?' said Kaz.

"Sure," said Mrs. Bates. "What?"

"We made a time machine together. . . . It's an incredible thing. Yet you've never wanted to take any credit for it. You're happy for me to be the inventor. . . . Why?"

There was a slight flicker of emotion across Mrs. Bates's features, so fast it was gone almost as quickly as it started. Then she smiled and said, "I have my reasons."

Kaz dropped the time machine by her side and said, "Well, I'm not going until you tell me."

Abigail sighed loudly, and folded her arms. "Here we go," she said. "Miss Dramatic!"

"Shut up, Abbey."

"Don't you tell me to shut up."

"For your information, Miss Smarty Pants, I'm doing this for both of us."

"Hey, you can leave me out—"

"Leave you out? But you're the one who started it. . . ."

The two sisters were warming up for one of their arguments, a spectacle Mrs. Bates had seen before. She spoke over the top of them, her voice strong and clear with authority. "Listen to me, both of you!" she said.

Kaz and Abigail stopped arguing to stare at her.

"You need to ask your father why I won't take any credit. When you see him," said Mrs. Bates, clasping her hands in front of her.

"Dad?" said Abigail. "What's he got to do with it?"

"That's why you two fell out, isn't it?" said Kaz. "He wouldn't give you any credit for your work in finding the cure for Miller's Syndrome."

Mrs. Bates didn't say anything in reply to the question, but her serene expression was enough for Kaz. How dare her father do that? Mrs. Bates had worked for him for years, and all she wanted was a little recognition, but he had shut her out. That was so typical of him. Nothing else mattered to him, and *no one* else mattered.

Kaz hugged Mrs. Bates around the waist, whispering, "Sorry." She wanted to say more. To tell her that she wasn't like her father. That she'd share the credit for the time machine . . . But Mrs. Bates prised her hands free and wiped away some tears from her eyes.

"Shall we do this, then?" she said, going to the tent flap to look outside.

"Okay," said Kaz, wiping her own eyes.

Mrs. Bates seemed to be staring at something for a long time; then she muttered, "Why are there so many police officers out there?"

"Oops," said Kaz. "We'd better go."

Abigail grabbed Kaz's arm, and Kaz inserted the fresh watch. Once again they were sucked back into the past.

13

Scene thirteen

They didn't waste any time, running immediately to their parents' house, hoping to avoid meeting anyone along the way. There were another Kathleen and Abigail living in this time, and the last thing they wanted was for someone to start seeing double. Luckily it was early in the morning, and there weren't too many people about.

The family dog greeted them enthusiastically as they arrived at their double-story, weatherboard home. Abigail gave him a rub behind the ears, then led Kaz round to a side window. They peered into their parents' bedroom window to see them frantically packing suitcases.

Kaz stared at these two adults. There they were, "Mum" and "Dad." She watched her mother, a tall, beautiful woman with deep auburn hair and angular features. Maryanne O'Bride had sharp eyes that could look right through you, yet she was as soft as a kitten in the right mood. Then there was her father, a distant, fiercely intellectual man who was always thinking about something else. You never interrupted him, not unless you wanted to get into trouble.

Looking at them now made her heart ache with a pain that felt real. *How could they have died on me? I was just a kid. I needed them.* Kaz wanted to rattle the windowpane and call out to them, but Abigail's voice brought her back to her senses.

"This is wrong," said Abigail. "They're already packing for their flight."

"That doesn't give us much time to stop them," said Kaz.

Abigail's forehead screwed up with tension as she stared at her parents. "We weren't meant to come this late," she muttered. "This must be Monday instead of Sunday. We missed by a day. They got the phone call late last night about the discovery on the island of Moltan."

"Right," said Kaz. "The discovery . . ." She racked her memory for what this discovery might be but came up with a blank. Common sense told her that it would have been linked to her parents' cure for Miller's Syndrome, otherwise why were they so excited? "Okay," she said, looking down at the time machine. "It's not a problem. We just take ourselves back a day and stop them from getting the phone call—"

Kaz stopped herself midsentence, and Abigail glared at her. "What?" she said. "What now?"

"I . . . I don't think my idea was such a good idea after all," said Kaz.

"Whoa. You mean the genius might have made a mistake?"

"It's not a mistake unless I actually make it," retorted Kaz with a sneer. "And I haven't made it yet. Let me think. Going back a day means using up this watch. That's not a problem as we can get watches from around here. . . ."

"So?"

"So," said Kaz through gritted teeth, "we've never tested this time machine using a watch from the past before. What if the time differentials don't match? What if the fuel is useless? We'd be stuck here forever."

"Oh," said Abigail.

Kaz's heart started racing. Time travel was a lot more risky than she ever realized. They couldn't go back. And now her parents were packing to fly to a tiny island where they'd make their final breakthrough in curing Miller's Syndrome. They'd send their report from the island, then fly home to a hero's welcome . . . one they would never see. Their return flight would crash into the ocean.

"Okay, we lost a day," said Kaz. "There's nothing we can do about that. We just have to take a risk, that's all. We'll have to go into the house and stop them."

"But . . . *we're* in there," said Abigail. "I mean, you and me a year or so ago . . ."

"I know," said Kaz. "So I guess that means getting rid of ourselves."

"You mean talking to the Kathleen and Abigail in the house?" said Abigail. Her eyes were wide with fear. "No," she said. "No way. We can't do it. The rules—"

"Forget the rules," said Kaz.

"What?" shrieked Abigail. "You can't just ignore the rules when it pleases you!"

"Why not? After all, I invented the time machine. So I guess *I* made the rules."

"Oh, that is so typical of you," snapped Abigail. "Pulling rank at a time like this."

"Someone's got to pull rank. You were going to allow Mum and Dad to catch the plane. . . ."

"I'm just being sensible," snapped Abigail. "Unlike you. Miss Genius, who won't let anything stand in her way."

"No, I won't," said Kaz. "Including horrible little sisters. So either come with me, or stay here and be a scaredy-cat."

"Who says I'm scared?" protested Abigail.

"Follow me," said Kaz.

She walked round the house to the back door. It wasn't locked, so she entered the house quietly, heading down a small corridor to her right. Somehow she knew her bedroom was along here. Abigail joined her as she opened the door. Kaz saw herself from the past at the wardrobe, looking for something to wear. The other Abigail from the past was putting on a pair of jeans. The two girls looked up, astonished to see themselves walk through the door.

"I'm sorry we have to do this," said Kaz. "I mean, we're breaking all the rules of time and time travel, but it's a matter of life or death."

She charged at herself, but the Kathleen from the past put her hand up and yelled, "Wait!" Kaz stopped. "I know how you got here," said Kathleen. "I finished the time machine, didn't I?"

Kaz nodded.

"What do you need to do?" said the past Kathleen.

"We can't tell you," said Kaz. "It's bad enough just being here, but telling you what's about to happen could blow time apart. Just trust us. We need you to vanish for a while. We can't take any risks."

Kathleen from the past speaks. "Okay, we'll do that."

Abigail from the past protests.
"No! I won't vanish. Why should I?"

Kathleen: "Come with me, little sister."
Abigail: "Ow, stop it! What are you doing . . . ?"

"We won't be long."

The past Kathleen put her hand on the wardrobe door and slid it closed. Kaz and Abigail heard the sounds of a brief struggle; then all was silent.

"Typical," whispered Abigail.

Kaz spun around on her sister to say something when the bedroom door opened and their mother walked in.

"Everything all right here?" she said. "I heard a noise."

"Mum," said Kaz, a tear starting to form in the corner of her eye. She wouldn't cry. After all, her mother hadn't died . . . yet. This was just an ordinary day, like all the other ordinary days in a person's life. But try as she might, she couldn't keep the tears away. As they flowed down her cheeks, she ran to her mother and squeezed her as hard as she could.

"I'll never let you go," said Kaz. "Never."

14

Scene fourteen

"But I don't understand, Kathleen," said Maryanne O'Bride, looking bewildered. "Only an hour ago you were as pleased as punch that we were going on this trip. You couldn't wait to be rid of us. Now you're pleading with us to stay?"

"I know it sounds pretty weird," said Kaz.

They were in their parents' bedroom putting forward a case to stop them from catching the plane. Kaz was doing all the talking, as Abigail had decided that since the "genius" was in charge, *she* could convince her parents. So far it wasn't working. Kaz had failed to come up with a believable reason why her parents should abandon their trip to the island of Moltan and *not* discover the cure to Miller's Syndrome, a cure they'd been working on for most of their professional lives.

There is no believable reason, thought Kaz. *This is hopeless.*

Thomas O'Bride paused in his packing and regarded his brooding daughter. So far he hadn't said a word, but this was not unusual. He could go for days on end without speaking if his mind was occupied by a work problem. He scratched his chin, then said, "Has anyone seen my pale blue shirt?"

"How can you think of your shirt?" yelled Kaz. "Our whole lives are at stake here!"

"We're only going away for a few weeks," said Maryanne O'Bride. "That hardly constitutes a whole life. And besides, if you want to look at it that way, *our* whole professional lives depend on this trip. You know that your father and I have devoted years to this cure. Now, after receiving the most promising news for nearly a decade, you want us to stay home? There's a child on this island who has recovered from Miller's Syndrome. That's never happened before, Kathleen. This child could hold the missing key to our research into the cure. We have to go."

"Can't someone else go?"

To everyone's amazement, Thomas O'Bride started laughing. He was not usually given to any sort of outburst. "Someone else?" he said. "And have them claim the cure that we have worked so hard for? This is *our* work, Kathleen."

"Your work!" shrieked Kaz. "Your work is ruining *my* life!" Wild, crashing thoughts and emotions overtook her and scrambled her reason. Everything she had ever wanted to be, everything she believed in, had been taken away from her by her father's work. How dare he do this? How dare they both just go off like this without a care for her? For their children?

"I hate your work!" shouted Kaz.

"Here we go again," said Abigail, sitting heavily on the edge of the bed. Her mother joined her, and her father decided that he too would sit out the tantrum.

A great, boiling rage flew through Kaz's brain. Jumbled, angry thoughts about not having money, about being neglected, about losing her TV, about wanting her parents to take notice of her. Kaz tried her hardest to push it all away so she could concentrate and say something meaningful.

"You've never listened to me," she eventually said.

"Now, that's not true," said her mother.

Kaz held her hand up, taking three deep breaths. "It is true," she said. "What about Mrs. Bates? I begged you not to cut her out of our lives—"

"Please don't mention that woman's name again," interrupted her father, a cold fury in his eyes.

"Oh?" sneered Kaz. "Why not? Because she reminds you how *selfish* you are? Always thinking about your precious work . . ."

Maryanne and Thomas O'Bride exchanged quick glances before Mrs. O'Bride spoke in as calm a voice as she could muster. "You have no idea what you're talking about, Kathleen," she said.

"Mrs. Bates was the only good thing in this family!" shouted Kaz, her anger boiling over again. "And you made her go away because you were jealous!"

Thomas O'Bride stood, his fists clenched by his side, his face white. "This has gone far enough," he whispered. "Now get out!"

Abigail stood up and joined her sister, having watched the genius struggle for long enough. "Look," she said. "Everyone calm down. We're just suggesting that you hold off for a while, at least until . . . um . . ." Her words froze on her lips. She couldn't say anything about the future that awaited her parents. That was a rule that they _knew_ could not be broken.

"Maybe it's time we finished packing," said Maryanne.

Kaz's shoulders slumped, and she turned to her sister. "Let's go."

They left the room quietly, with Thomas O'Bride more concerned about where his socks were than what his daughter had just said.

They don't even care, thought Kaz as they headed back to their own bedroom. Their past selves emerged from the wardrobe on Kaz's signal and sat on the beds. Each girl stared at her own image, still startled by being in the room with herself.

"Well?" asked Kathleen from the past.

"We can't say anything," said Kaz. "All we can tell you is that it's not going very well."

"Good," snapped Abigail from the past. "Maybe you can leave now?"

"You see?" said Kaz, turning to her own-time little sister. "You see what a brat you are?"

"I am not!" protested Abigail.

"No, she's not," added the other Abigail, standing with her double. "Or I'm not . . . or whatever."

Kathleen stood and came over to Kaz, searching her face for clues as to what was going on. "I wish I could help you," she said.

"I know," said Kaz. "Maybe we could talk with Mrs. Bates . . . but no. That would just scare her."

"She's away," said Kathleen. "Besides, you know how much Mother and Father dislike her."

Kaz relived the cold emptiness of her life after Mrs. Bates had been banished. It didn't seem right that this woman would mean more to her than her own mother and father. The same uneasy feeling came to her. She remembered her first time trip with Abigail, back to when the statue was being erected in the park. A mysterious person had been talking to the police officer. There was something familiar about that person. . . . Kaz felt the doubt grow much stronger than a mere nagging. It chewed away at her.

"Something's wrong," whispered Kaz.

"What is it?" asked the three girls.

"I don't know."

The two Abigails rolled their eyes simultaneously and sat on the bed with a flounce. Then they looked at each other and started laughing.

"Look at them," said Kathleen. "The mutual admiration society."

Kaz smiled at her duplicate sister. There was a knock at the front door, and they heard voices. Their aunt had arrived to babysit the girls for the period that Maryanne and Thomas would be in Moltan.

"Okay," Kaz said to the other Kathleen and Abigail. "You two say your goodbyes and act normal. Abigail and I will have to keep trying."

The past Abigail stood and left the room with her older sister. The other stayed with *her* older sister.

"What's the plan now?" said Abigail.

"We hide in the car," said Kaz, looking down the hallway to see if the way to the back door was clear.

"And then?"

"I don't know!" shouted Kaz, tears forming in her eyes. "I haven't got answers for everything. It's too hard."

There were too many variables at play here: the past, the future, her doubts, her emotions . . . and something else. An important task . . . Everything depended on it.

There's a . . . a bad guy. Yes, I have to find the bad guy . . . somewhere.

Kaz's heart started racing, as if she'd woken to realize she'd slept through an important exam. What was she missing here? A clue? A fleeting thought came to her but vanished as fast as it had appeared. Kaz wanted to scream with frustration, but she knew that wouldn't help. There was only one way forward now: stop her parents getting on that plane. She had to ignore the doubts, the voices, and the dim memory of another life in another place.

She looked at her sister. "Now," she said. "We do it now. Stop them. Or we've failed."

Abigail placed her arms around Kaz and held her. "Maybe we accept that we've failed," she said. "We could just pull out."

For a brief moment Kaz felt the relief of Abbey's suggestion. Pull out, go back to where they belonged, and just accept the past for what it was. Then she remembered someone telling her it was time that girls flexed their muscles and took charge. Who had said that to her? Mrs. Bates? Whoever it was, that was exactly what she needed to do right now—be strong, push through this mess, and *make something happen*!

"No!" said Kaz, a grim determination on her face. She pushed Abbey away. "We do not pull out. I'm not a quitter."

"But you said something's wrong. . . ."

"This is our chance, Abbey," said Kaz. "We have to change the past."

"Shouldn't we stop to think about it?"

"There's no time to think. I'm going. Now!"

Abigail huffed with frustration, then followed her older sister. They made their way to the car, doubt dragging their mood down into a dark gloom. Was someone meddling with them? Who could they trust? Kaz knew she had to do what she'd come here for. How could she live without her parents, especially after seeing them alive again?

Nobody could ask her to give that up. Nobody.

15

Scene fifteen

Inside the O'Brides' car, the brilliant scientists drove to the airport. But they did not realize that two stowaways were lurking in the backseat. Thinking that they were alone, Maryanne and Thomas discussed their troublesome daughter.

"Why can't you tell Kathleen how much you love her, Thomas?"

"I guess because she's so much like me. . . ."

Kaz: "Dad . . ."
Thomas O'Bride:
"What the . . . ?
Aaaarrgh!"

 "My leg! My leg!"

Thomas O'Bride's cries could be heard for blocks all around. As people came running and an ambulance was called, Kaz sat by her father and held his hand, telling him that it would be okay.

"The island," he said. "We'll never get there. Maryanne, you go. . . ."

"Don't be ridiculous," said his wife. "I'm staying with you until the ambulance comes."

"There'll be another time to go to the island, Dad. When your leg is better." *And you won't catch the flight that crashes into the sea.*

Abigail tapped her sister on the shoulder and led her away from the dramatic scene.

"We have to go," she said.

"But what about Dad . . . ?" began Kaz.

"This isn't our time, Kaz. You know that. What will we do when they discover there's a Kathleen and an Abigail back home?"

Kaz looked at the scene before her and sighed. Yes, their time here was over. They'd done it, saved their parents' lives. She tried to tell herself that everything was a success now. To forget the nagging feeling from before that something was wrong. How could this be wrong? It was what she'd dreamed about all along.

"Okay," she said. "It's time."

There was only room in the ambulance for Maryanne O'Bride, so she gave her daughters money for a taxi to meet them at the hospital. After they watched the ambulance drive away, Abigail ran to a phone booth and dialed home, filling her other self in on what had happened. Then she returned to Kaz, nodding to indicate it had all been arranged. The real Kathleen and Abigail were going to take the bus to the hospital and meet their parents there. It was time for Kaz and Abigail to go forward in time again to where they belonged.

The two girls slipped behind a tree with the time machine; then Abigail held Kaz's arm as she pressed the Now button.

Once again they were flung across the dimension of time.

16

Scene sixteen

Kaz was thrown to the ground the second she returned to her own time. She lay there, a little dazed, then looked around. She was at the site of the car crash, only it was a year later. There was very little evidence of damage to the tree her father had smashed into. Kaz stood up and tried to get her bearings. They were at least several blocks from the town square.

"Come on, Abbey," she said.

There was no reply.

"Abbey?"

Kaz wheeled around, but her little sister wasn't there. Then she realized that she no longer had the time machine either. Had she dropped it midtransit? Or had Abbey wrenched it from her? Whatever, she couldn't waste time trying to work it out. She ran for the square. By the time she reached it the crowd had thinned to only a few people.

We must have been gone for quite a while, thought Kaz. All the tents had been packed up and taken away, as well as the stalls and band equipment. *This doesn't make sense. No time should have passed while we went into the past.*

A few people were gathered around the statue, and Kaz ran toward it. As she approached, she saw that something didn't add up. The statue in front of her was not a statue of two people. Only one person stood on the base, a proud, intelligent look on her face.

"Mrs. Bates?" whispered Kaz.

Underneath the statue were the words, "Julienne Bates, who discovered the cure for Miller's Syndrome and saved thousands of children."

What the heck is going on here?

Kaz was aware of a buzzing of voices growing around her, and she looked up to find strange faces looking at her with expressions of outrage and anger.

"How dare you just show up here like this!" said one woman.

"Me?" said Kaz. "But I . . . I live in this town. . . ."

"Call the police," said a man.

"Now, wait on," said Kaz.

"No need to call them," said another voice. "Here they are."

Kaz turned to see the Irish policeman approaching her with Abigail at his side. *Good. Abbey can sort out this mess.*

"Where have you been?" asked Kaz.

"Why did you do it, Kathleen?"

"Do what? Abbey?"

"Come along now, Kathleen. We won't have you attempting to murder anyone else. . . ."

"Murder? No!"

 A word came to her, strange, incongruous, but she shouted it anyway. "Cut! Cut!"

And her whole world spun away once again.

17

Scene seventeen

Kaz stared at the TV screen, her heart racing. It was as if she'd just woken from a crazy nightmare, and had to work out what was real. She was Kaz, not Kathleen. This was her world. Kaz tried to calm her breathing, looking around at the viewing room. Once again she was in the library at good old Capra Video High School. Back in her ordinary, real life. Not some time-travel movie where she changed the past. But try as she might to convince herself that it had only been a movie, vivid images from the Vidz flashed through her brain. How could she have been accused of attempted murder? Unless . . . in changing the past she had made bad things happen too. Really bad things.

Kaz ran the last scene through her mind. Why had the statue been of Mrs. Bates? Had she gone to the island instead of her parents? But if she did discover the cure for Miller's Syndrome, why didn't she share it with Thomas and Maryanne O'Bride?

Unless they hated each other so much it became impossible to share, thought Kaz. That had to be it. The bitterness between her Vidz parents and Mrs. Bates wasn't going to vanish overnight, especially not if Mrs. Bates discovered what they'd been searching for all their lives.

I bet Mrs. Bates even offered to share with them, thought Kaz. *But Dad would have said no.*

Kaz wanted to go back into the Vidz and shake her father. How could he be so stupid? Why couldn't he just accept that Mrs. Bates owned some of the limelight for the discovery of the cure? Sometimes she really hated her father. . . .

Whoa! What am I doing? He's not my father. My dad is at home helping some men carry the furniture out to a truck!

Kaz stood up, then sat down again. This Vidz was far more complicated than Hamish's had been. All he'd had to do was swing a big sword and knock a few goblins on the head. She sighed, gathering her things into her bag. Time to try and find Hamish and Bo again. Surely they were at school by now.

I still don't really know who the bad guy is, thought

Kaz. *And I don't know how it's all connected to my world here at Capra. What a mess.*

Kaz pushed the Eject button on the DVD player to retrieve her Vidz, but another movie popped out.

"What's this?" she muttered. "Where's the Vidz?"

She peered into the DVD slot. It was empty. What was going on? How could her Vidz vanish like that? She started to panic, thinking she must have dropped it without noticing. For ten minutes she searched under the table, through her bag, and in every corner of the room. There was no Vidz.

The school bell rang, and Kaz picked up her bag. She was tired after being in the Vidz. She'd get Hamish and Bo to help her find it later. Right now she had to get to home-group or she'd cop a late notice. As she ran from the library, she saw that it was now empty. Mrs. Leigh was nowhere to be seen. A man was filling in behind the desk. *He must be new,* thought Kaz. She hadn't seen him before.

"Hi," she called as she hurried out.

"Hi, Kaz," replied the man.

My reputation precedes me.

The air was still oppressively hot, and it hit Kaz like a blast from an oven as she headed for her home-group. Bo was waiting outside the room, leaning with his back against the wall and one leg up. He was typical Bo, not a care in the world, not even bothered by the heat. Kaz felt like running up and kissing him. After being in the crazy Vidz and traveling back and forth in time, it felt so good to see a friendly, familiar face.

"Bo," she said. "A weird thing just happened. No,

two weird things. First I lost my Vidz. Second, some stranger knew my name . . ."

She stopped. Bo was paying no attention to her. He was watching one of the other students—a brash know-it-all named Kelly—stand behind one of the shy kids whose name Kaz couldn't remember. Most of the class were kept amused by Kelly as she mimicked the quiet kid's every movement.

Normally Kaz would have said something to Kelly, told her to grow up, but there were more important things on her mind.

"Bo," she said. "Look at me. I need your help. My Vidz is missing."

Bo turned to her, a strange expression on his face. He just stared at her.

"What?" said Kaz. "What's your problem today?"

"I could ask you the same question," said Bo. "What the heck are you talking about?"

"My Vidz. I lost it. . . ."

"What vid? Your video exercise?"

"Bo! Stop being mental! I lost my Vidz. Oh, and I haven't told you. It's me, Bo. I entered the Vidz. . . ." Her voice trailed off as she caught the look on Bo's face. Either he was playing some dumb game with her, or he was mad about something. This was useless. She didn't have time for games. "Where's Hamish?" she asked.

Bo shook his head, then picked up his bag. "I'm going in," he said. "At least the inmates in here don't talk nuts *all* the time."

Kaz followed him in. Maybe he was angry with her for not ringing Hamish last night. But that hadn't been her fault. Her dad had been so stubborn about the air-conditioning, it had just made her see red. . . . Kaz paused, remembering Kathleen and all the arguments she had with her parents. She could see them and Abigail lined up on the bed, waiting for her to finish her tantrum. Was she like that here in the real world, too?

The teacher started reading out the names for roll call, and Kaz looked over to see Hamish sitting by himself near the window. She gave him a wave to say hi, and he quickly turned his head away. Kaz shrugged. Okay, that had to be it. He was still mad at her for yesterday, and Bo was mad too. She leant over toward Bo and whispered, "What has Hamish said to you about me?"

Bo looked at her with that strange expression again and shook his head.

"Come on. I'm not stupid, you know. When I said hello to him just then he ignored me. . . ."

"What would you wanna bother with that guy Hamish for?" asked Bo. "Man, that kid's so quiet I don't think I've ever heard him speak!"

"Bo!"

Bo glared at her and whispered, "Could you please *not* talk to me for the rest of the day? Okay? Because you are acting very weird."

Weird? Me? What about you?

As she listened to the teacher read out the call sheet, which was their daily notices bulletin, a cold, sick feeling started to creep into her stomach. Everything was weird, that was for sure. But could it be . . . ? Was it because everything had *changed*?

Kaz stood abruptly.

"What's the matter, Kaz?" asked the teacher.

"I . . . I gotta . . . Sorry, but I have to go."

She ran from the classroom, ignoring the protest from the teacher and the queer looks from her classmates. She *had* to know for sure what was going on. Her legs carried her effortlessly across the street, down the main drag, and along more streets until she came to the suburb where her father's factory used to be. If everything was okay, then the factory would be a closed-up building with a notice out front saying the business had gone broke. . . .

There was noise coming from the factory. Its roller doors were open to allow air to flow through on this stinking hot day. Kaz could see men working at the machinery as they made the metal sheets and parts that her father's business manufactured . . . no, *used to* manufacture! Some of the men waved to her as she came to the door. She knew them, but the last time she'd seen them they'd had long faces and worried expressions. They'd just lost their jobs.

Two men were standing in the aisle of the factory between the massive machinery, laughing, sharing a joke. One was her father. He looked so happy, so relaxed. Kaz hadn't seen him so carefree since . . . since the factory went broke. But this wasn't a shut-down factory. This was a fully running business, and standing next to her smiling father was . . . him! Cushing! No, he was in jail. He stole money from the school. He stole money from her father. Without even thinking through what she was doing, Kaz marched up to them both. Cushing was talking to her father about a new girlfriend. Kaz couldn't believe the way her father just stood there smiling. Didn't he realize what a crook this man was? They hadn't noticed her yet, continuing with their easygoing conversation.

"Yes, she's blond. Did I mention that?" said Cushing.

"You happened to mention it about ten times," said Kaz's father, laughing.

"And she loves going to the movies. In fact, she knows more about them than me. . . ."

Kaz groaned. She never knew that Cushing was a movie freak. That was even more reason to despise him, for moving in on her territory!

Must be why he took the job at Capra High after Dad's business went bust, thought Kaz.

The machinery roared around her, a loud reminder that her father's business had gone bust in another time, another reality. Now that she'd meddled with the past, it was doing fine. Had she stopped Cushing from taking money from her father? Or was he just smarter about it now? Only taking smaller amounts? Kaz shook her head. Cushing was rotten through and through; there was no way he'd stop his evil ways. All she'd done was stall him.

Kaz's father turned from the conversation to notice his daughter standing there.

"Oh, hello, darling," he said above the noise of the machines. "Everything okay?"

"No, it's not," said Kaz, pointing to Cushing. "I can't believe you're being nice to this creep."

"I beg your pardon," said Cushing, going red in the face.

"Well, you don't have it," said Kaz. "You're a liar and a thief. . . ."

Her father grabbed her by the shoulder and shook her roughly. "Kaz! What do you mean by saying things like that?"

"Dad! Don't you understand? This guy is bad. I know what he's up to—"

"You apologize to Mr. Cushing at once!" shouted her father.

"No, I won't," Kaz shouted back at him. "You never listen to me. Never!"

She ran from the factory feeling sick. Bo had been right, you couldn't go meddling. Cushing never sent her father broke, which meant he never went looking for a job at Capra Video High School as the bursar. And that meant he didn't get around to blackmailing the principal. There was no danger to Capra High, no money illegally bet on the races. There was no evil at play in the school when the old Vidz director tried to hand over the Vidz to Hamish.

Kaz stopped, fighting a dizzy, nauseous feeling. Hamish never received the Vidz, never entered the knight movie to slay the lair-goblin and defeat Dudley. He was still just that quiet kid in the corner.

Kaz tried not to cry. What good were tears now? She had to work out what to do. The bad guys would start winning, and winning, and winning until happy endings were just a thing of the past.

As she walked up the main street, her mind lost in a myriad of thoughts, Kaz spotted a newspaper banner that made her heart sink.

GANG OF TEENAGE ZOMBIES STRIKES FEAR IN CITY!

What? A gang? It was only a couple of kids before . . . before I meddled with the past. It was getting worse, and she'd made it possible. She had to go back into the Vidz and change the past in the movie so that everything would become normal again.

And that's when the horrible realization hit her. There was no movie to go back to. Hamish had never handed her the Second Director's Vidz. That was why it hadn't been in the DVD player. She was no longer Kaz Murneau, Second Director.

The Vidz crew didn't exist.

Scene eighteen

In a run-down, deserted part of the city, a lonely figure contemplated her future.

Kaz is stuck in a torment of her own making.

Everything is lost.

Unless . . .

19

Scene nineteen

It took Kaz the rest of the day to find him. She had to ask a heap of questions around the school, then take a peek at the student records when the secretary wasn't looking. All she had was a first name to go by, and a vague description that Hamish had once given her, but eventually she tracked him down.

It came as no surprise that Michael was working as an usher at one of the big cinemas in the city. Where else would a graduate of Capra Video High go to earn some cash? Except this was no ordinary graduate—this was the First Director before Hamish. This was the student who had handed over the Vidz and started their amazing adventures. . . . Well, he would have been that student, if Kaz hadn't mucked up the past.

She watched him take people's tickets, a bored expression on his face. He was her one and only slim hope of getting back into the Vidz movie. If he'd never gotten the chance to hand the four Vidz DVDs over to Hamish, then maybe he still had them.

As the last of the customers dribbled into the theater, Kaz approached Michael, rubbing her hands over her jeans nervously.

"I need to talk to you," she said.

"You can get tickets at the foyer," said Michael.

"About the Vidz . . ."

He glared at her, his eyes wide for a telltale second; then his face went blank. "I don't know what you're talking about," he muttered.

"Yes, you do," said Kaz. "I'm a student at Capra. Up until very recently I was Second Director of the Vidz crew."

Michael pushed past her and said he was busy, but she grabbed him by the elbow and spun him around. "Listen to me," she hissed, her face close to his. "I've mucked everything up. I went into a Vidz and changed the past. That's why you couldn't hand over your Vidz. I changed everything. You probably looked for the right person but couldn't find him. Or maybe you did talk to him. . . ."

"No," said Michael quietly. "I never found my successor."

"His name is Hamish," said Kaz. "He's the First

Director . . . or should be. I was Second, Bo Third, and Fourth . . . I don't know."

Michael stared at her, holding her gaze intently, searching for any lies behind her story. No one else in the world would know about the four Vidz directors, unless they *were* a Vidz director.

"What do you want from me?" he said. "I'm too old to enter a Vidz now. That's the way it works. . . ."

"No, I don't want you to enter the Vidz. I have to go back, but I don't have a Vidz anymore. I need the ones you never handed over."

Michael sat on a seat with his head in his hands, his shoulders slumped. He stayed like that for some time, and Kaz sat next to him, wondering what had brought on this awful gloom. *Maybe he threw the Vidz out*, she thought with alarm. Eventually Michael sat up straight and looked at Kaz.

"I remember clear as day when the old First Director handed me the four Vidz, all those years ago," he said.

"How many Vidz crews have there been?" asked Kaz.

Michael shrugged. "Don't know. My crew were amazing. We fought our way out of some pretty terrifying situations . . . or perhaps I should say movies."

"Vidz," suggested Kaz.

"Yeah." Michael smiled. "It was such an honor . . . and a huge responsibility, knowing you were fighting evil and not being able to tell anyone else about it. When our time came to stop being the Vidz crew and hand over to the next, I had one last task to complete. All I had to do was make sure that the Vidz lived on . . . and I failed."

"You haven't failed," said Kaz, placing her hand on his. "You just might have saved everything."

Michael nodded. "Let's hope so," he said, leading her to the back room where the staff stored their personal belongings. He opened a locker and removed a large envelope.

"I keep them with me all the time," he said. "Just in case . . ."

"Just in case someone like me turns up?"

He nodded, shuffling through the DVDs. "Which number did you say you were?" he asked.

He was holding the First Director DVD in his hand, and Kaz had a momentary urge to snatch it, be number one, be the leader of the crew. Then she remembered all the barbs from her Vidz little sister, all the complaints about how she had to be the center of attention. There was a truth in that for both Kathleen and herself. She did always want to be Kaz the Popular. Wasn't that why she hated being poor?

"I'm Second Director," she said, and Michael handed over the DVD.

Kaz felt like singing with joy. She was back in the game now, and this time she intended to make a happy ending. All she had to do was nail down the bad guy in the Vidz . . . or bad gal . . . or whatever it was! She'd use the genius of her Vidz character somehow, and she'd learn to think about the big picture and not just what she wanted.

"These Vidz," said Kaz. "When you were First Director, did they, you know, teach you stuff about yourself?"

Michael smiled. "Oh yes," he said. "All the time."

"Mm," said Kaz. "And was it stuff you sometimes didn't want to learn?"

Michael laughed. He patted Kaz on the back and wished her good luck. She stood on tiptoe and gave him a quick kiss on the cheek; then she ran.

20

Scene twenty

She was the character again, Kathleen to everyone else, Kaz to her sister. *And* she was about to be arrested! Abigail had a hand on her arm, and the policeman was about to grab her as well. This time he didn't have some friendly advice or useful information for her. No, his intention was clear: to throw her in jail. *Not today, Officer. I've got work to do.* Like find another time machine somehow, throw herself back into the past, and fix things up!

There was no way she could do that behind bars.

Abigail's grip started to hurt, and Kaz looked her sister in the eye. There was so much anger there, so much hatred. Had it all stemmed from that time in the bedroom when Kathleen had locked her in the wardrobe? Or was it deeper than that? How could a sister turn against her so harshly?

"Abigail," Kaz whispered through clenched teeth. "Please . . ."

"You ruined everything," said Abigail. "Everything . . ."

"Why do you hate me?" shouted Kaz. "I'm your sister!"

There was a momentary hesitation in Abigail's expression. "You're a hopeless sister," she whispered, loosening her grip. Kaz had a mere second to act before the cop grabbed her, and she didn't waste any of it. With a push against her sister's chest, she ran in the opposite direction, heading straight toward a bus that was about to pull away from the stop.

"Please!" shouted Kaz to the driver, who had the doors shut.

The man sighed, then opened the doors for her, shut them again, and pulled away, leaving the policeman and Abigail in his wake.

Kaz sat on the bus and thought everything through. She was still Kathleen, a genius child, but she'd changed the course of time and history and messed everything up. Now she didn't have a time machine because she'd never got to finish building it. One year before, her father had gone to hospital with a broken leg. Mrs. Bates had gone to Moltan instead and discovered the cure for Miller's Syndrome, which meant she hadn't been around to help Kathleen build the time machine. So for the past year

Kathleen, Abigail, and their parents had had to watch Mrs. Bates receiving awards on TV, Mrs. Bates in the newspaper. And all the while, both girls knew that the strange visit from the other Kathleen and Abigail had made all this happen. No doubt this had made the war between herself and her little sister worse. Abigail would have wanted to tell someone about the strange visit, but Kathleen would have stopped her.

Kaz saw her family's house flash past and got off the bus at the next stop. As she walked back, she wondered who was home. She knew now that her parents hadn't died in the plane crash. Were they involved in the attempted murder?

The dog greeted Kaz at the gate, licking her hand. "Doesn't look like you've had many walks lately, fella," she said as she headed for the garage.

Could that be because her father's leg was still bad? Or because he was in jail? Kaz wished she knew more, but at the same time she was afraid to learn the truth. The word *murderer* was haunting her.

Somewhere in the garage an incomplete time machine lay hidden. It was her little secret. No one else knew about it, not even Mrs. Bates. Everyone assumed there was just the one time machine, but Kaz had built this one for backup. The original time machine might be in the house, or it might have been destroyed by someone close to her. Someone evil . . . Kaz racked her brain and found she could picture the second time machine nestling in its hiding spot. By now she was used to these character memories from the Vidz entering her head as if they belonged to her. In fact, everything about being the character of Kathleen had a comfortable feel about it.

"Aha!" said Kaz, removing a locked metal box. She found the hiding spot for the key without even thinking about it, and pulled out the nearly completed time machine. It looked almost perfect, except there was no aerial. Kaz sat with the machine and tried to remember what they'd used for the aerial.

The image from the fortune-telling tent came to her, of Abigail stilling her hand, telling her how fragile the aerial was. They'd taken months and months to find the right material. And in the end it had been a carbon-based material with a silvery sheen to it. But what would make that? So many things were carbon based.

Kaz closed her eyes, exhausted by the chase and the struggle to remember. Her mind drifted from thought to thought and finally stopped on a quiet moment she had had with Abigail. She could see it, could flash back to it, reliving it as a scene from a movie, her private memories of her sister.

21

Scene twenty-one

INT. KATHLEEN'S BEDROOM, NIGHT

KATHLEEN is brushing ABIGAIL's hair. The younger
sister sits in a chair before the mirror, relaxed.
Kathleen stands behind her, brushing Abigail's hair
carefully. This is a soft moment between the two
sisters, who normally fight like cats and dogs. The
lighting is muted, warm.

> KATHLEEN
> You have such lovely hair, Abigail.

ABIGAIL
Mm . . . thanks.

Kathleen continues to brush, and Abigail stares at her in the mirror.

ABIGAIL
Do you remember how you'd brush my hair all the time when I was little?

KATHLEEN
Yes.

ABIGAIL
You don't do it so much these days.
How come?

KATHLEEN
Too busy, I suppose.

ABIGAIL
With that time machine?

KATHLEEN
Shh. Dad'll hear.

Abigail sighs.

ABIGAIL
Why is everything so complicated now?

Abigail looks up at her sister, but Kathleen is not paying attention. She has a strand of Abigail's hair in her hands.

> KATHLEEN
> This could be it!

> ABIGAIL
> Could be what?

> KATHLEEN
> The material for the time machine's aerial!

Abigail groans.

22

Scene twenty-two

Kaz entered the house cautiously, looking around. No one was home, so she ran to their bedroom. Sure enough, Abigail's pillow revealed a beautiful, long strand of hair.

But the aerial had some kind of silvery covering. . . .

She went to Abigail's dresser and found what she was looking for—silver nail polish! Kaz painted the hair and strung it between the two arms on the machine. At least her sister could help her in this way. A quick search through her own dresser revealed a ready supply of watches, and she stuffed a handful into her pockets. Now she needed some dates.

There was a pile of newspapers stacked neatly at the back door. Kaz sat down next to them and carefully flicked through the pages. It took forever, and time was running out. Sooner or later Abigail and the cop would turn up. After flicking through a myriad of pages, she found a newspaper from a few days before, with the headline she'd been after:

BATES MURDER ATTEMPTED AT CEREMONY

Her heart missed a beat as she scanned the article, snatching brief details: ceremony—pier—drowning—attempted murder! Reading the date quickly, she wound the dial on the time machine to the day before the article, and was sucked back in time. As soon as she arrived she ran to the pier, where a ceremony was about to begin. In just moments Mrs. Bates would uncover a statue of a dolphin to commemorate all the children who had died from Miller's Syndrome. Kaz pushed herself forward through the crowd until she could see Mrs. Bates. She was standing at the end of the high pier. Then something unexpected happened.

Kaz watches the famous Mrs. Bates throw roses into the sea in memory of the children.

Thomas O'Bride has other ideas. "You evil fake!"

The real Kathleen tries to stop her dad.

A terrible tragedy.

Kaz ran back to the house, tears streaming down her face. Behind her, the tragedy continued to unfold. Her real self from this time was in the water, swimming, desperately searching for her father, who was nowhere to be seen. His leg was still weak from the accident, and he couldn't keep himself afloat.

Her father had drowned.

That's twice I failed to save him, thought Kaz. *Abigail is right. I'm a hopeless big sister . . . and a hopeless daughter.*

She arrived back home, pressed the Now button on the time machine, and was returned to the present. Kaz didn't even bother to look around when she was back in her own time; she just sat on the back step and hung her head in her hands. What a total mess she'd made of everything. Her father was dead after all.

Could there be any way to change time for the better? Or would it always end up a twisted mess? Kaz took a deep breath, wiped away her tears, and was about to stand on her shaking legs when a voice snapped at her.

"Thought I'd find the *genius* at work here!"

It was Abigail.

"Oh, Abbey," said Kaz. "I don't have the energy to run anymore." She looked around expecting to see the policeman and was relieved to find that he had not accompanied her sister.

"Constable O'Leary will be here later," said Abigail, reading her thoughts. "I put him off for the moment. . . ."

"Thank you."

"I didn't do it for you!" shouted Abigail. "You are so self-centered, you think everything revolves around you."

"Okay, okay," said Kaz, standing on tired legs.

She picked up the time machine, but Abigail lunged at her and wrenched it from her hands.

"Give it back!"

"Where did you get this thing?" asked Abigail.

"None of your business, Abbey. Now give it back so I can get on with the job."

"What job?" shrieked her Vidz sister. "Ruining everything?"

"No, doing what I came here for in the first place . . ."

"No way!" shouted Abigail, holding the time machine above her head. "Not again. I'm going to smash this one like I smashed the other. Before it causes any more harm."

"Please," begged Kaz. "Please don't." She felt so weak, how could she stop her little sister? "I have to do what I'm here for. . . ."

"It's always Kaz, isn't it?" said Abigail with a sneer. "Kaz who has the important job. Kaz the Popular. Kaz the one everyone wants to be friends with. And in the meantime I don't exist."

Kaz looked at Abbey. Could she be the bad guy? The evil she had to defeat? If she smashed this time machine, then everything was ruined. Kaz lunged at her sister, but Abigail was able to push her away effortlessly. The run to the pier and back had drained Kathleen of energy. "You can't do this to me," she said. "You're my little sister. I let you in on everything. . . ."

"You don't even talk to me. Nobody does. I hate that. All the quiet ones are ignored, and now it's worse after you changed time. . . ."

Kaz stared at Abigail. What was she talking about? *All the quiet ones are ignored? Where are they ignored? Nobody talks to her.* Kaz remembered Hamish in the home-group, how timid he'd looked. And the way everyone had just watched Kelly be mean to that quiet kid without saying a word. *Me included!* Then Kaz saw a girl with pale hair . . . just like this girl in the Vidz. A girl with silver nail polish. Was this really Abigail talking, or . . . or *Abbey*?

"You're from Capra High," whispered Kaz.

"Of course I am, you idiot!" shouted Abbey. "You've been back and forward in time with me and you never once recognized me. I recognized you straightaway, because you're the famous Kaz, who everyone talks about. I'm nothing. . . ."

"Hold on," protested Kaz. "You have an American accent. Plus, you're wearing glasses. I mean, your character is wearing them, and the real you doesn't wear glasses. That makes it a bit difficult to recognize you. . . ."

"Oh, I'm Superman and Clark Kent now, am I?"

Kaz smiled weakly. Abbey had a good sense of humor, even when she was angry. "You were in the library," said Kaz. "When I started watching the Vidz."

"What's a Vidz?" asked Abbey.

Kaz ignored the question, sitting down again. This new development was going to take some getting used to. Abbey still had the time machine poised above her head, but Kaz couldn't raise the energy anymore to try to stop her. If she was from Capra, then she definitely was not the bad guy.

"Can you imagine what it was like for me?" said Abbey, still towering over her. "I'm in the library doing homework, then *wham!* Suddenly I find myself in some strange dream, or movie. Can you imagine how scared I was? And then you burst into the tent, only you didn't know who I was. I almost said something, but I was scared it would . . . I don't know . . . make me stuck in this thing. I really needed you to help me out, but you were weird, like you were acting or something. So I decided to just go along with it . . . and Abigail sort of took over."

"Yeah," said Kaz. "That happens. This *is* some kind of movie . . . sort of a magical movie. You start out playing a character, until, well . . . the characters are very strong."

"And then it all stopped," said Abbey. "Twice! The first time I was back in the Capra High library and you ran out from the viewing room. I yelled at you to stop, but you completely ignored me!"

"Oh," said Kaz. "I remember someone calling to me. . . ."

"That was me!" shouted Abbey. "I was so frightened. I went outside to get myself together. I was just convincing myself it was a weird nightmare, when *wham!* I'm in the movie again! And you still didn't know me, so I played along and we went back in time. . . . Then everything went *really* weird in the movie before I . . . I . . ."

"You came back to Capra High again," said Kaz.

"Yes, but it wasn't *my* Capra. It was some horrible place where everyone was mean to each other, especially to the shy ones like me. I thought it was bad before you changed time, but it was ten times worse after. And it was all because of this horrible machine, wasn't it? You changing time in this movie changed time at Capra, too."

Kaz nodded, impressed with Abbey's ability to work it all out.

"Please sit down now," said Kaz. To her relief, Abbey sat, placing the time machine on the step between them. Kaz didn't make any moves for it; there was still a lot to be said. She gave Abbey a full explanation of the Vidz then, how the bad guy had to be defeated. She explained that the Vidz worked as a mirror reflecting bad things in the real world. She was about to tell Abbey about the Vidz crew, but she paused. For some reason she couldn't bring herself to say what was obvious—that Abbey was the Fourth Director. Abbey was smart, and she had plenty of courage. . . . Instead, Kaz gave her a vague explanation of how she'd come to have this amazing video that could catapult you into a realistic, evil-fighting movie.

I'll tell her later, when she's ready.

"What do we do now?" asked Abbey. "I mean, I have all these strong feelings about you. I hate you . . . and yet I don't hate you. I'm angry with you. . . . I don't know if my sanity is gonna cope with all this."

"Tell me about it," said Kaz with a sigh. "What we do is finish this movie, and that means defeating the bad guy."

"Oh?" said Abbey. "And who is that?"

"I'm sorry," Kaz said. "A minute ago I thought it

might be you. Now . . ." A thought came to her about the so-called attempted murder. She looked at her schoolmate and Vidz little sister. "You accused me of attempted murder before. Why?"

Abbey went red in the face and looked away. 'They told me you did it . . . tried to murder Mrs. Bates. I guess I wanted to believe it. After all, I hated you. . . ."

"Who told you?"

"The police . . . O'Leary . . . and Mrs. Bates."

"You've talked to her?"

"I think so," said Abbey, a confused expression on her face. "Or maybe my character did. . . . I don't know anymore."

"You or your character, it doesn't matter here in the Vidz," said Kaz. "It's all real."

Abbey turned to Kaz and squeezed her arms tightly. "She was heartbroken, Kaz. Like, sobbing. Couldn't understand why you tried to kill her—"

"I didn't!" shrieked Kaz. "I was trying to stop Dad!"

"That's not what she said."

"Abbey, I saw it. I went back in time and saw it. I *did not* try to murder her."

"Then why would she . . . I mean . . ."

Kaz stood and instantly felt dizzy. She propped herself up against the side of the house. Some heroine she was, head spinning, mind confused, accused of murder. Then she smiled. Wasn't this just like the end of the second reel in a movie? The heroine comes to her darkest hour, when everything looks bleak and miserable. When the whole world is against her. And then she comes up with a brilliant plan. And that plan was . . .

Kaz sighed. Her head was completely empty. *So much for the second-reel climax. Looks like this movie is going to be a bit different.*

"Constable O'Leary was trying to help you," said Abbey, staring at her shoes.

"Huh?"

"At the square that day, when he was chasing you. I don't think he was trying to stop us from using the time machine, he was trying to tell you something about Mrs. Bates. He told me he'd done checks on her past and there was something not quite right about her. But now that she's the one who discovered the cure, and you tried to kill her . . ."

"I was stopping Dad!"

"Whatever. Now he thinks *you're* the criminal. . . ."

"Oh, does he?" snapped Kaz. "So I'm the bad guy, eh?"

What did she do now? Go back to when she was born and try to fix things? Every step turned up a blind alley. Maybe there was no bad guy in this movie. Maybe it was all a big joke. Kaz smiled. Hamish wouldn't see it as a joke. He'd tell her to try harder. She remembered the fight she'd had with him over bad guys and bad gals. She'd sneered at him then because he knew so much about film history. He'd looked at her and said, "But Kaz, history is everything. If we don't know what's been done by the great filmmakers before us, how can we ever know if what we make is any good?"

At the time she'd passed it off as another of Hamish's annoying comments, but maybe there was something to it. History *was* everything, especially in a time-travel movie . . . or a Vidz! Kaz racked her brain, going over all the significant dates in her Vidz history.

"Abbey," she said, "does your character remember when Dad and Mrs. Bates had their big argument?"

"Yes," said Abbey. "May twenty-second, on my . . . Abigail's birthday. It was the afternoon. I remember because all I could think was what a horrible birthday present it was. Why?"

Kaz bent down and picked up the time machine, winding back the dials. Abbey stood and joined her.

"What's this gonna prove?" she asked. "All you'll see is Dad going psycho at her."

"So?" said Kaz, her resolve crumbling by the second. "It's all I've got at the moment."

"Okay," said Abbey.

Kaz slid a watch into the slot, and they went back to the day all the troubles began.

23

Scene twenty-three

They could hear the screaming the minute they returned. Both girls snuck round to the window of their father's laboratory and looked inside to see Thomas O'Bride standing in front of Mrs. Bates, his face red, his veins sticking out, shouting at the top of his voice.

"I trusted you. I allowed you into my family . . . and you betrayed me!"

Mrs. Bates seemed fairly calm, considering that this man was yelling in her face. She talked quietly, slowly, trying to soothe the furious Thomas O'Bride.

"I really don't know what you mean, Thomas."

"You copied the secret files," shouted O'Bride. "You were stealing my notes on the cure to Miller's Syndrome."

"I haven't copied anything."

"But I saw you just now. I saw you!"

"Please," said Mrs. Bates. "I was just looking for you. Search me if you like. I haven't stolen anything from you."

Thomas O'Bride threw his arms in the air and said he wouldn't search her because she'd already hidden what she took.

"And where have I hidden these supposed copies that I made?" asked Mrs. Bates, gesturing around the laboratory.

"I don't know," said Thomas O'Bride.

"This is your lab, Thomas. Look around, but I can assure you that there's nothing to find because I haven't made any copies of your secrets."

"But you did . . . I mean . . . I saw you. . . ."

Kaz turned to Abbey, a look of shock on her face. Never had she seen her father so unsure of himself. Inside the laboratory, Thomas O'Bride had gathered himself and was now pointing at the door.

"Get out," he said.

"But Thomas . . . the girls, they mean so much to me . . ."

"Out!"

Mrs. Bates held her head high in defiance, then walked slowly out of the room without a backward glance.

Abbey and Kaz stayed silent for a moment or two, watching their father quietly sobbing in his laboratory, showing more emotion in those few minutes than they'd ever seen him show in their entire lives. Then he walked out.

The two girls turned to each other again, fear in their eyes.

"This doesn't prove a thing," whispered Abbey.

"I don't get it," whispered Kaz. "If she did steal files, where are they? She never came back for them. . . ."

All they'd seen was their father being totally unreasonable and Mrs. Bates being thrown out for a crime there was no proof of. She didn't have anything hidden on her. That was obvious. Thomas O'Bride had made a huge mistake.

Kaz felt like screaming in frustration. Was she ever going to find the bad guy in this movie? Just when she thought she might know, she saw a scene that proved otherwise.

"It's just like Mrs. Bates told me," said Abbey.

"Mrs. Bates?" asked Kaz.

"Yes," said Abbey. "She said to me if I ever had any doubts about whether she was telling the truth, just go back and see what Dad did to her."

Kaz stepped away from the house, her heart racing. *Why would Mrs. Bates say that? Unless . . . Of course!* That had to be it. She fumbled for the time machine, her fingers clumsy with nerves.

"What are you doing?" asked Abbey.

"Don't you think that's a bit too . . . neat?" whispered Kaz.

She took her sister's hand, then wound the dial back ten minutes. The short trips were the worst, whipping back through such a tiny space of time. Their heads spinning, they moved forward to look into their father's laboratory window once again.

Kaz and Abbey watch a figure inside their father's lab.

Who is copying the secret files?

Mrs. Bates.

And she has her *own* time machine.

Kaz and Abbey watched Thomas O'Bride enter the room. He had just enough time to take in the scene at the photocopier. He saw Mrs. Bates with the secret files. And he might also have noticed her with the time machine, too, before the secret files suddenly vanished from view. Of course, Kaz and Abbey knew what had happened. Mrs. Bates had slipped back in time to remove the evidence, then reappeared with an innocent expression on her face. It happened in the blink of an eye.

"That's how she did it," said Kaz as the argument began inside the laboratory. "She used her own time machine to go to a time when she could sneak the files out."

"So Dad was right. She *did* steal his secret files. . . ."

"Yes," whispered Kaz, ejecting the used watch from her time machine. "'It's the final reel now, and this climax is going to be a doozey!"

24

Scene twenty-four

It was such an ordinary intersection, just a spot where two roads met, and yet this was a significant place in the history of Kathleen and Abigail O'Bride's family. This was where their father drove off the road and into a tree after getting a fright from seeing his daughters in the backseat of the car. This was where he broke his leg, so that he couldn't go to Moltan, allowing Mrs. Bates to step in and claim credit for the cure he'd been working on for so long. One year before, his history had been altered by two girls with a time machine. And now they were going to try to rearrange history again, to change time and hopefully to get it right with this attempt.

Abbey emerged from the phone booth smiling, returning to her Vidz sister with her thumb up.

"She bought it?" said Kaz.

"You bet," said Abbey. "Told her you were ready to hand yourself in. She was all care and concern. 'Tell Kathleen I'm coming.' As if she was our mother . . ."

Abbey's words trailed off as she saw the look of pain on Kaz's face.

"That's the thing, isn't it?" said Kaz. "She *was* like a mother to us. . . . I feel it so strongly."

"Me too," said Abbey, sighing.

"How can that be?" asked Kaz. "I know it's because the character takes over, but, I mean, how can I almost love someone when she's so . . . evil?"

"Maybe that's the way life works," said Abbey. "Maybe it's not always so easy to pick the bad guys. . . ."

Kaz smiled at Abbey's phrase. Everyone was so used to saying "bad guys" that it rolled off the tongue without any effort. And yet Mrs. Bates was exactly what Kaz had been searching for in the library, a woman in a movie who was totally bad, totally evil. A bad gal. Not a femme fatale who got a man to do most of her dirty work. Not a tragic dame who did wrong because of love or passion, but a manipulating, scheming woman who wanted fame and power and was prepared to do *anything* to get them. Even split up a family.

"You know," said Kaz, "if I was going to pick a family that was ripe to be split apart and manipulated and have its children wind up trusting a stranger more than their own parents, then I'd pick our Vidz family, wouldn't you?"

Abbey nodded. "Yep," she said. "As far as families go, I'm glad my real parents back at home love me. I might complain sometimes, but they're nowhere near as bad as what Abigail and Kathleen have to put up with."

Kaz winced, remembering the shouting arguments with her dad over the stupid TV and DVD player. As if anything like that actually mattered now. She'd take her dad over Thomas O'Bride any day. Her father loved her and gave her time when she needed it. She'd never complain about her life at Capra again. Kaz thought about Bo, her oldest friend, and about Hamish, so knowledgeable and so reliable. Then she looked at Abbey.

Why didn't I tell you about being Fourth Director? she wondered. *Could I be jealous? Or did Kathleen take over?*

It was wrong to hold back that information. Wrong to keep Abbey from the Vidz crew. That was just as bad as splitting up a family.

"There's something I've got to tell you," said Kaz, touching Abbey lightly on the arm.

But she didn't have a chance to continue. A car pulled over at the intersection, and Mrs. Bates emerged.

"There she is," whispered Abbey.

Mrs. Bates had a large bag over her shoulder, and Kaz smiled, guessing what might be inside. She stepped out from behind the tree with her sister, leaving her backpack on the ground. Abbey placed a firm hand on Kaz's elbow and marched her toward Mrs. Bates. Kaz hung her head, trying to look defeated, exhausted. Mrs. Bates leant back against her car, waiting.

"This is no good," whispered Kaz. "We need her closer."

"I know," said Abbey.

They arrived at the middle of the intersection, and Kaz dug her heels in, stopping still.

"Come on!" shouted Abbey.

"No!" shouted Kaz. "I've changed my mind."

Mrs. Bates stepped away from her car, but she was still by the side of the road.

"Well, that is very typical of you, my dear Kathleen," said Mrs. Bates. "Stubborn to the end. It's a fine trait, but it will get you into trouble later in life."

"I call it determination," said Kaz. "Something you taught me, Mrs. Bates."

The woman laughed, nodding at Kaz's jibe. "Yes, you could call me determined," she said. "Still, it's better than being like your father, totally distracted all the time. Couldn't even see what a brilliant young daughter he had . . ."

Kaz felt the words sting her, and she closed her eyes. *No! Don't let her do this.*

"Sorry," said Kaz. "But that isn't going to work anymore. You might have been able to drive me away from Dad in the past, but I'm different now."

"Is that right?" said Mrs. Bates. "You're different? Ha! You're nothing but a spoiled, snotty little brat who has a tantrum whenever she doesn't get her own way."

"Shut up!" yelled Kaz.

Abbey jerked her Vidz sister by the elbow and whispered, "Cool it." Then she looked at Mrs. Bates and said, "Can we just get this over with? She's said she'll turn herself in, so let's drop the dramatic, tearful movie scene, okay?"

"Very well put, Abigail my dear," said Mrs. Bates. "What do they say? Let's cut to the chase. Only there's no need for a chase, because my quarry is here."

To the relief of the two girls, Mrs. Bates walked out into the intersection to where they stood. At last, they had her where they wanted her. Kaz tensed. This was the final moment. They had to act fast or everything would be ruined. Mrs. Bates took Kaz's hands in hers and smiled her kindest, warmest smile. Kaz felt like being sick.

"This is for the best, my dear. You'll see that one day. . . ."

"All I can see is a bad gal," whispered Kaz. Then she turned to her Vidz sister and nodded.

Everything happened so fast. Kaz twisted her hands around to grab Mrs. Bates by the wrists as Abbey ripped at the bag, pulling it down from the woman's shoulder onto her arms, where it acted as a rope, binding her.

"Stop it, Abigail!" shouted Mrs. Bates, pulling against Kaz's hold.

"Hurry!" shouted Kaz. "She's strong!"

Abbey unzipped the bag and saw what they'd hoped would be inside: Mrs. Bates's time machine. She pulled it out, wound back the dial one year, and looked at Kaz.

"The watches? Where are they?"

For a brief second Kaz panicked, then she remembered where the supply was. "My pocket!" she yelled as Mrs. Bates struggled and twisted against her. "Ow! She's hurting me!"

Abbey tried to extract a watch from Kaz's pocket, but all the twisting and pulling was making it nearly impossible.

"Keep still!" she cried.

"Are you crazy?" yelled Kaz.

"Come on, now, girls. This is really very silly. . . ."

At last Abbey had her hand in Kaz's pocket and found an elusive watch. But Mrs. Bates was clever, and she twisted Kaz around, squeezing Abbey's hand against Kaz's hip and trapping her.

"Pull her back!" shouted Abbey.

"I can't. . . . She's dug in!" shouted Kaz.

It was a stalemate. Without the watch, they couldn't send Mrs. Bates back in time and complete their plan. Now what? Stand in the middle of the road like this forever? Then Kaz saw the answer.

"On her wrist!" she shouted, and nodded at Mrs. Bates's watch.

Abbey smiled. The watch had a leather strap, easy to undo. She had only the one hand free, and used it to fiddle with the watch as Mrs. Bates kicked out at her. They looked like a bizarre circus act, each locked onto the other, turning and twisting round and round in the middle of the road. Mrs. Bates had to maintain the lock on Abbey's hand, Kaz had to hold her grip, and Abbey had to use her left hand to try to get the strap free.

Something had to give.

"I did it!"

Mrs. Bates screamed with frustration as Abbey held up her watch, a huge grin on her face.

"No, Kathleen," she whispered. "Don't do this to me. . . ."

"My name is Kaz," said Kaz, grinning in the woman's face. "And I make movies."

She shouted, "Now!" and pushed back against Mrs. Bates, releasing her grip. At the same moment, Abbey slid the watch in and stepped back. There was a brief whoosh of wind as Mrs. Bates vanished; then the two girls were left standing in the middle of the road, alone.

"Quick!" shouted Kaz. "Let's get back there."

They ran to the tree and grabbed their time machine, winding back the dial a year and inserting a watch.

They had to see if their plan worked.

25

Scene twenty-five

At the intersection, one year before, a car approached with Thomas and Maryanne O'Bride inside. They were on their way to the airport. Their daughters were at home. And *this* time the two daughters from the future were outside the car instead of inside!

The way is clear for Thomas O'Bride to drive through.

Watch out!

The tires screech. . . .

26
Scene twenty-six

By the time the police had taken all the statements, it was getting dark. The O'Brides had missed their flight to Moltan, but they could get another one the next day. A police car drove away with Mrs. Bates in the backseat, a look of fury on her face. "I hate that family!" they could hear her yelling. "They should have died in that crash!"

Thomas O'Bride put his arm around his wife's shoulder. "That was scary," he said. "I knew that woman was bad, but to try and make us crash. . . ."

Maryanne nodded, still shaking. "When she was standing there, and the car swerved . . . I thought about our girls. How much I'd miss them if I couldn't be with them."

"I thought about them, too," said Thomas.

He took his wife's hand. "We still have them," he said softly. "After Moltan, I'd like us to get together as a family and work a few things out. I want the fighting to stop."

"Me too," said Maryanne.

Most of the witnesses had gone home by now. They'd reported to the police that they'd seen Mrs. Bates deliberately step out in front of the O'Brides' car as it approached the intersection.

"It was like she came from nowhere," said one man.

After hearing the eyewitness reports, as well as some of the history between Mrs. Bates and the famous scientists, the police decided to take the woman in for questioning. It didn't help that she was yelling at the family with such obvious hatred. Eventually the police would hear what Constable O'Leary had found out, that there was a shady past to Mrs. Bates. It would all add up to prove that she had a motive to attempt to hurt the O'Brides.

Two girls watched the drama unfold from behind a tree. They stayed out of sight, a strange machine in their hands. The darker girl turned to the fair-haired girl and smiled.

"Looks like we've done what we needed to do here," she whispered.

"Are you sure this will work?" whispered the other.

"I mean, it was their flight home from the island that they died in."

The dark-haired girl thought for a second or two, then said, "They've been delayed by a day. That will mean they come back a day later and miss the fated flight."

"Hopefully."

"Only one way to find out."

They looked at the strange machine, pressed a button, and vanished into thin air.

27
Scene twenty-seven

Kaz and Abbey had decided to go straight to the O'Bride family home rather than pass by the square to check the statue. But when they arrived home, it looked exactly the same. Had time been changed? Surely their parents would be inside. . . .

The family dog was lying on the front doormat, looking exhausted. Had he been for a walk? Who could have taken him? He looked up, wagging his tail, making a comical thumping noise on the front door. It sounded as if someone was knocking. The door opened and

Maryanne O'Bride was standing there, smiling at her daughters.

"Did you get it?" she asked.

Kaz and Abbey looked at each other. *Get what?* They shrugged and Maryanne rolled her eyes, then smiled at them.

"Honestly, you two. You live your lives with your heads in the clouds . . . or should I say in movies? After all, you watch enough of them. I sent you to the shops to get milk? What did you buy?"

"Er, nothing," said Kaz, looking over her Vidz mother's shoulder inside the house. Was Thomas there? Had they succeeded?

"Is that Kathleen and Abigail?" came a deep voice. Thomas O'Bride stood behind his wife, a letter in his hand. "Perfect, girls, your timing is impeccable. I've just received a letter."

"Oh?" said Kaz, walking behind them into her Vidz home.

She looked around for clues as to what had happened over the past year. Everything seemed normal enough, except for one detail. Her parents weren't distant and distracted like they usually were. In fact, they almost seemed normal. Thomas O'Bride sat on the leather couch and waved his letter at the girls, but they weren't paying any attention to him. There was a framed award hanging on the wall behind the couch, an award for the O'Brides, who had discovered the cure for Miller's Syndrome.

They'd done it.

"They're going to have a one-year celebration for

us," said Thomas O'Bride. "For the cure. And it's in Sweden. How about that? So your mother and I want you both to come, of course. . . ."

"Sweden?" said Kaz. "Cool."

"I've never been to Sweden," said Abbey.

Maryanne O'Bride laughed and gave her daughter a playful punch on the arm. "You are so silly sometimes."

"Of course you've been to Sweden," said Thomas.

"Yes," said Kaz, winking at Abbey. "Of course we've been. You know, Nobel Prize . . . ?"

"Oh," said Abbey. "Yes, the Nobel Prize thingy . . ."

Thomas stood and came over to Kaz. "Kathleen," he said. "How are your calculations going for the time differentials? I'm very interested in your experiments."

Kaz felt the time machine in her bag, weighing heavily. Should she tell him? Or leave time alone for a while?

"Not so good," she said. "You know, time is a tricky area."

"It is?" said Thomas. "I'd love to discuss it with you."

"Oh, I've moved on," said Kaz. "I'm now looking at different, er, dimensions. You know. Different realities."

"Go on," said her father, a look of pride beaming on his face.

"Like how one world can seem real, and another can seem like . . . well, like a movie."

"Fascinating," said Thomas O'Bride.

The phone rang, and Maryanne answered it. "It's Sweden," she said.

The O'Brides went into their study to take the call.

Abbey sat on the couch, but Kaz couldn't relax. She knew what was coming, and she felt curiously sad about it.

"What?" asked Abbey, seeing Kaz's agitation. "We've done it. We beat the bad guy, and by the looks of it, got this family back together again."

"I know," said Kaz. "It's time to leave."

"For good?" said Abbey.

Kaz nodded, and Abbey stood. She had a nervous look on her face again.

"Back to Capra," she said.

"It'll be different there," said Kaz. "Just ask Hamish."

"'How do we do it?" asked Abbey.

"Say 'Cut!' and you're out."

"Wish I'd known that earlier!" Abbey said. "Hey, isn't it going to be a bit weird when the real Kathleen and Abigail get back with the milk?"

"They're smart girls," said Kaz with a smile. "They'll figure something out."

Abbey yelled, "Cut!" and was gone. Kaz took one last look around, and was about to yell "Cut!" when she remembered that she still hadn't told Abbey she was Fourth Director. Never mind, it would be good for the whole group to let her know.

With the framed award on the wall filling her with pride, Kaz yelled, "Cut!" and knew that the credits would be rolling.

28

Scene twenty-eight

It took Kaz several explanations before Hamish and Bo were finally able to grasp the full impact of what had happened in the Vidz. They were sitting in the canteen before school started, the day after Kaz had been taken to the world of the O'Brides. It was just the three of them, the old crew. Even though Kaz had asked Abbey to come early, she hadn't shown up.

"That is pretty amazing," Hamish kept saying. "We knew the Vidz were powerful, but to actually change time in the real world. Wow!"

"So, like, in this other time thingy, I thought you were crazy, did I?" said Bo.

"Yes, you did," said Kaz, punching him on the arm. "You were horrible to me."

"Ow!"

Hamish was deep in thought, pondering everything Kaz had said. He gave his two friends a distracted smile, and they paused in their antics to look at him.

"What?" asked Kaz.

"This isn't as easy as last time," he said. "We knew Cushing was the bad guy. We have no idea about this one . . ."

"Yes, we do," said Kaz. "Someone we all trust. Someone who is dividing kids from their families."

"But all those zombie teenagers hated their families anyway," said Hamish.

"He's got a point there," said Bo. "You shoulda heard about this Jason dude's family. They put him away."

"Well, that fits with my Vidz family. When we weren't fighting, we weren't talking to each other."

"Still doesn't lead us to the bad guy here in the real world," said Hamish.

Kaz's happy mood fell into a dark pit. Hamish was right. They were nowhere near catching the real bad guy. What had that Vidz been about if evil still flourished in the real world?

They sat at the table like three gloomy monkeys, lost in their own thoughts. They didn't even notice when a shy student approached them. She stood near them expecting they might greet her, but when no one spoke, she shrugged and turned to leave.

"Abbey! Sorry, I didn't see you there," said Kaz. "Sit down and meet the crew."

Abbey sat and was introduced to Hamish and Bo, even though she knew them from her classes. Kaz kicked Hamish under the table, and he coughed, pulling an envelope from his bag.

"Um, Abbey, there's something that Kaz *forgot* to tell you. . . ."

"What?" said Abbey, her nervous expression coming back.

"Relax," said Hamish. "This is a good thing . . . when you're not fighting hags and goblins."

"Just tell her," said Kaz, rolling her eyes.

"Abbey," said Hamish, "you are the fourth Vidz director. You are part of the Vidz crew."

He handed her the envelope. "Welcome," he said.

Abbey removed the Vidz DVD and looked at it in awe. Her name was written on the cover and disk in flowing writing: "Abbey Chauvel, Fourth Director."

They cheered when she received her Vidz, and Mrs. Leigh came out of the library to investigate.

"Having a party, then?" she asked.

"Sorry," said Kaz. "We're kind of celebrating. . . ."

Mrs. Leigh caught a glimpse of the Vidz before Abbey stuffed it into her bag.

"That one of ours?" she asked.

"No," said Abbey. "It's something I . . . um . . . made."

"Oh, well, don't forget to give me a copy when you can for the student archive. I love watching your little movies." She smiled at them all, then gave Kaz a significant look. "Kaz, how's things?"

"They're good, Mrs. Leigh," said Kaz, blushing a little.

"Your movie problem is solved, then?"

"Yes," said Kaz. "I think it's got a happy ending. . . . Well, almost happy. The credits aren't quite rolling yet."

The librarian held Kaz's gaze, saying nothing, then shook her head. "No," she said, "I can see there's still a scene or two left. Have to keep my eye on you."

Then she left them to return to the front desk.

" 'Keep an eye on you?' " said Bo. "She's so cool, she even talks like a movie."

Kaz laughed. "Do you think if you watch too many films then everything you say will sound like dialogue?"

The others laughed at this suggestion, except Hamish. He was lost in thought. Kaz looked at him and asked what was up. Hamish shrugged. "I don't know," he said. "It might be nothing."

That raised their curiosity immediately. They badgered him until he finally relented.

"It was just that, well, Cushing said exactly the same thing to me," said Hamish. " 'I'll have to keep my eye on you.' It was just weird, that's all. You know, that Mrs. Leigh should say it too."

"Is that all?" said Bo. "For a moment I thought you'd worked out who the bad guy was."

Now Kaz was lost in thought, ignoring their chatter. Eventually she said, "Maybe Hamish *has* worked it out."

"What?" asked Hamish.

"When I returned to Capra, the other Capra, where everything had changed . . . I saw Cushing in the factory with my dad. Anyway . . . I don't know . . . he was talking about his new girlfriend who knew heaps about movies."

"So?" said Bo.

"He said she had blond hair. . . ."

They all turned to look at Mrs. Leigh, her flowing, film-star blond hair standing out under the library's fluoro lights.

"Nah," said Bo. "It couldn't be."

"Why not?" asked Abbey. "Remember how much Kaz and I loved Mrs. Bates?"

"But," said Bo, "Mrs. Leigh is cool. . . ."

"She said a strange thing to me," said Kaz. "She invited me to come to her cinema when she thought I was having family troubles. . . ."

Kaz didn't reveal that she really was having a bad time with her family. She wasn't ready to let go of being popular Kaz.

Hamish sat forward when Kaz told them this, his eyes alert. "She invited you to her cinema? But she deliberately told Bo and me not to come. . . ."

"Because she didn't think you two had family problems," said Abbey quietly.

The group turned to look at Abbey, nodding.

"So . . . ," said Bo.

"It fits," said Hamish. "That Jason kid, he lived near her cinema. Maybe that's where she . . . she does things to their brains. . . ."

"Oh yeah? Like, how?" asked Bo.

The First and Second Directors shrugged, but the Fourth Director had a keen look in her eye.

"Subliminal images," said Abbey.

"Sub-what?" said Bo.

"Subliminal images. You know, like during the film you flash in a quick frame or two of a message, so fast the eye can hardly see it. 'Drink more milk!' or something like that. I wrote an essay on it for film history. . . . It kinda works like hypnotism, but you'd have to believe a bit in the message for it to convince you."

"Hm," said Hamish. "That's impressive. So maybe Mrs. Leigh shows special movies . . . with an evil message."

"Like, 'Steal your mum and dad's money,'" whispered Bo.

"Yeah, but why?" said Kaz. "I mean, what's she going to get out of brainwashing a few teenagers into stealing their parents' money? Sounds a bit far-fetched . . ."

"Hey, Kaz has got a point," said Bo.

"Hm," said Hamish. "Unless it's just the test run."

"What?"

"Hamish is right," said Abbey. Then she blushed and wouldn't go on until they'd urged her to. "Don't you see? If you can brainwash people by showing a special movie . . . Imagine how many people you could get to when you were confident it was all working. Thousands and thousands of people go to watch movies every day. . . ."

"Man, we've gotta stop her," said Bo.

Hamish had gone a pale color and seemed to be almost shaking.

"You okay, Hamish?" asked Kaz.

"Yes," he said in a whisper. "I just had this thought. What if all the evil here at Capra . . . What if it was organized? Cushing knows Leigh. . . . And they know . . . ?"

They sat quietly for a moment, each of them going over what Hamish had just said. This was huge now. Not just an isolated few teenagers. Kaz broke the silence.

"I'll go and accept her invitation to visit her cinema," she said.

"It could be dangerous'" said Hamish.

"No way 'could,' man," said Bo. "It *will* be dangerous."

"Then I'll need all of you to help," said Kaz. She stood and went over to Mrs. Leigh, her legs feeling wobbly. Somehow trapping Mrs. Bates had been a lot easier than this, but the trap had to be set. The good of her own world depended on it.

29

Scene twenty-nine

In a strange little cinema on the other side of town, a girl entered alone. She was greeted by the woman with the film-star looks, then sat in the dark.

Another teenager watches the show.

But the message doesn't get through.

The subliminal frame is stopped, and now everyone can see the evil.

But the bad gal escapes!

"After her!" shouted Hamish.

The four Vidz directors ran out into the street, but Mrs. Leigh had vanished into the hot afternoon.

"How could we lose her like that?" said Bo.

"At least we've stopped her brainwashing," sighed Kaz.

"But we haven't stopped her," said Abbey. The others nodded in agreement.

"She'll be back, all right," said Hamish. "The bad ones always come back. . . ."

30

Scene thirty

Later that day, Kaz waited until her father was coming up the path to the front door before bursting out with the bunch of flowers. "Surprise!" she yelled.

"What are these for?" he asked.

"It's an apology thing," said Kaz. "Because I was a total jerk. . . ."

"No, you weren't," said her father. "You were just disappointed, that's all."

"I had no right," said Kaz.

"Okay . . . well, this is obviously a day for surprises. I've been to the secondhand dealers. I got a bit of insurance money. . . ."

"And?" said Kaz,

"And," said her father, "it's not new, and it's not the best ever made, but if you look in the backseat of the car . . ."

Kaz rushed to the car and peered in, her heart thumping.

Now she could play her Vidz at home.

A home she was *happy* to live in.

Kaz had what every Vidz director needed. In fact, what every kid needed. Not a TV or DVD player, but a family who cared about her.

She smiled, because the music was playing, the credits were ready to roll, and the happy ending was finally coming through.

Fade out . . .

About the author

Ian Bone began writing books for young people in 1993 and has had more than twenty-five titles published, including *The Song of an Innocent Bystander* (short-listed for the 2003 Children's Book Council Book of the Year award), *That Dolphin Thing, Tin Soldiers* (short-listed for the 2001 NSW Premier's Award), and *Fat Boy Saves World*. His books have been published in the United States, the United Kingdom, Korea, and Germany, and six of them have been listed as Notable Books by the Children's Book Council of Australia.

Just like his Fast Forward characters, Ian Bone loves movies, has studied film history, and knows way too much about strange and obscure films. Ian has always wanted to create a book that would combine great storytelling with video techniques. When he was awarded the Carclew Fellowship in 2000, he used the time to develop the Fast Forward series. He says there's a little bit of him in each of the Fast Forward characters. He still gets a thrill when the lights go down in the cinema and the main feature begins. And yes, when he was young, he wished he could live his life in a movie.

Ian lives in Adelaide, Australia, and is currently writing more titles in the Fast Forward series.

About the illustrator

Jobi Murphy is a freelance designer and illustrator who has worked on numerous books for Random House in Australia, including *Muddled Up Farm, Max Remy: Superspy, The Saddle Club, Pony Tails,* and the Fast Forward series. She was also responsible for designing Blake Education's award-winning *My Alphabet Kit*.

Despite being discouraged from mixing her colors by her second-grade teacher, Jobi fulfilled a longtime ambition when she began working in children's publishing. She now divides her time between illustrating and designing children's books and enjoying time with her husband and their baby son in the bushy Sydney suburb of Grays Point.

Fast Forward #1: A Dangerous Secret

Hamish's life should be perfect now that he's at Capra Video High School. But then he finds a note in his locker that says, "You have been chosen to fight evil!" He enters the world of Vidz, where a happy ending is more than just pretty music over the credits. There's no script to go by, no manual to read. Hamish must defeat the evil goblins and hags in the Vidz, or evil will grow in the real world. He must make sure the good guys win, or there'll be nothing good left when he returns. . . .

Available now!